*Cowboy J. D. McCoy's
first words:*

**Upon learning he was going to be
a temporary dad:**
"What?!"

Upon seeing baby Jessie:
"I can tell by the way she's hollering that girl's a
McCoy for sure!"

Upon seeing Rebecca Chandler:
"Damn, she's pretty. Does she come with
the kid?"

Upon falling in love with Rebecca:
"You'll never get the 'L' word out of me!"

Dear Reader,

Who doesn't love a wedding? And if you're single, you just naturally start thinking about your own love life and who you might someday end up with. So is it any wonder that when Morgan Cutler, the heroine of Marie Ferrarella's *A Match for Morgan*, starts making the rounds of all her siblings' weddings, she finds herself thinking a few thoughts of love? What amazes her, though, is the identity of the man she's thinking about. She and Wyatt McCall have been at odds ever since she can remember, so why is he suddenly looking awfully…kissable? You'll hate to say goodbye to THE CUTLERS OF THE SHADY LADY RANCH, but I think you'll agree with me that this miniseries is going out with a real bang.

Then check out Lynn Miller's *Did You Say* Baby?! Take one cowboy who knows *nothing* about babies, add one heroine with a baby in tow and no working knowledge of cowboys, stick them together in one suddenly-too-small house out on the ranch and…boom! Spontaneous combustion is bound to occur. This is only Lynn's second book, but she knows her stuff, and you'll be looking forward to more from her, I promise.

So have fun, and don't forget to come back next month for two more wonderful Yours Truly novels, the books all about unexpectedly meeting—and marrying—Mr. Right.

Yours,

Leslie Wainger
Executive Senior Editor

Please address questions and book requests to:
Silhouette Reader Service
U.S.: 3010 Walden Ave., P.O. Box 1325, Buffalo, NY 14269
Canadian: P.O. Box 609, Fort Erie, Ont. L2A 5X3

LYNN MILLER

Did You Say Baby?!

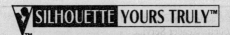

Published by Silhouette Books
America's Publisher of Contemporary Romance

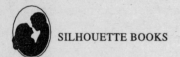 SILHOUETTE BOOKS

ISBN 0-373-52088-3

DID YOU SAY *BABY?!*

Copyright © 1999 by Lynn Miller

Dear Reader,

I have a great fascination with competent people. Especially when those extremely competent people are thrown into unfamiliar situations and discover they haven't a clue! I can relate to people who hold down demanding careers, have families and maintain extracurricular activities without missing a beat, but underneath it all, they have dust balls the size of gophers under their beds, have to buy new dolls because they can't figure out how to put the arms back on the old ones after their kids pull them off, and always—*always*—make the dinner portions too big, because they can't divide the fractions in the recipes. Yes, ma'am, those are my kind of people. I like to write about them because of the humor I see in their lives. After all, if you don't have a sense of humor about life—you're missing the joke!

So I started asking myself, *What if?*

What if you take one baby abandoned on a stressed-out single woman's doorstep, then add a sexy, stubborn cowboy who's more at home with cows than babies, and stick them on a ranch together in the middle of a small town in Texas. What do you get? Well, that's what I wanted to know. So I had to write *Did You Say* Baby?! to find out!

I hope you enjoy all that I discovered about single women, cowboys and babies!

All the best,

Lynn Miller

1

I'm no good for this baby right now. I need a week
or so to settle something. Take her to my brother,
J. D. McCoy, in Wildwalk, Texas.
He'll know what to do.

                                                        Rosalie

Rebecca Chandler refolded her client's note and stuck it
back into the pocket of her simple, tailored suit jacket. She
stared through the window of her rental car and sighed as
she took in the slightly dilapidated ranch house before her.
Regardless of what Rosalie McCoy had told her about her
childhood, Rebecca still couldn't think of a ranch in Texas
without imagining something ostentatious—a home out of
an old television show like "Dallas" or something. She
chuckled at her own naiveté.

*What did I expect—a sprawling mansion and a tall,
handsome cowboy who looks like he owns the world swaggering up to sweep me off my feet? Get real, Rebecca!*

The two-story ranch house in front of her had no connection with the one in her imagination, unless one counted
the color of the walls, which might be white under that
layer of dust. It was hard to tell, with the low angle of the
setting sun casting its golden glow over everything. Biting
her lip, Rebecca told herself to stop avoiding the issue. It
didn't really matter what the house looked like. She had a

job to do. She was here to deliver Rosalie's baby to the child's uncle. Then, after making sure the baby was settled, Rebecca would take off to enjoy the rest of her first vacation in four years.

That decided, she glanced in the rearview mirror at the pink-cheeked baby who was finally sleeping soundly in the rear car seat. The poor little thing hadn't slept a wink today and was probably exhausted from traveling. Rebecca watched the baby for a second more then pushed her hair back from her face and opened her door to face the reality of summer in Wildwalk, Texas. She gasped as the heat hit her. Reluctantly, she stepped out of the air-conditioned car. It was rarely this hot in Boston. She shook her head, letting her well-styled hair curve around her chin, then straightened her shoulders under her light khaki-colored suit and opened the back door. Undoing the restraining strap from around the baby, she lifted her from the car and cooed, "Come on precious, time to see your new home." Arranging the light blanket over the sleeping baby she now cuddled in her arms, Rebecca turned to face the house. Hesitantly, her stylish heels sinking into the gravel with each step, she picked her way across the driveway to the verandah that ran the width of the house.

She sent a silent plea to the sunset sky above her. *I hope I'm doing the right thing.* To put a six month old baby in the hands of a man she'd never met was probably insane. But she had no choice.

In the corral off to the side of the barn, J. D. McCoy sat at ease on his favorite horse. His long, lean body rose slightly from the well-worn saddle as he studied the sporty looking red car that had pulled to a stop in front of his home. He pulled his hat down farther over his eyes to shield them from the leftover sunlight which seemed determined to pierce his tanned skin. Squinting, he strained to recognize the woman behind the wheel. He wasn't expecting company, was he? Although it wouldn't be the first time a woman had decided to track him down, ostensibly to take pity on his bachelor household with home cooking. Then to offer anything else he might have a yearning for. His lips quirked. Come to think of it, some of those offers had been mighty tempting…too tempting sometimes for a man who didn't trust women farther than he could throw them.

Bringing his attention back to the car, J.D. hooked his knee around the saddle horn and waited to see what would happen next. He was a man who lived to take action, but had been taught by experience that sometimes it was better to hang back a bit and study the situation first instead of going off half-cocked. Then he saw the "situation" extend a high-heeled shoe, attached to a long, elegant leg, followed by a trim body in a suit that made her look as cool as sherbet. The vision was topped off by a shining cap of dark hair that glinted with blue-black sparks in the setting sun. His mouth watered at the sight and something tightened in his gut.

By God, it's been a long time since I've seen a woman who packed a punch like this one.

Intrigued, J.D. forgot all about playing it cool and cautious. Instead, he straightened his leg and slid to the ground. After all, he didn't have to trust women to enjoy them. With a soothing murmur, he patted his horse, looped the reins around the pommel and strode to the fence. In two moves he was over the top railing and striding toward the porch. A beam of sunlight hit him in the eyes so he couldn't quite make out what she had in her arms, but he didn't care. He was more curious to know if she had as big an impact on him close up as she did from thirty yards away.

At the jiggle of metal and the scrape of footsteps on gravel, Rebecca turned from the screened door, stained brown with years of weather and dust, to peer at the source of the sounds. She hugged the baby closer to her and her jaw dropped as she took in the image walking across the gravel drive toward her.

A cowboy.

An honest-to-goodness cowboy was swaggering toward her with the slightly bow-legged strut of a veteran horseman wearing toe-pinching boots. He looked much as she'd imagined—tall, lean and as if he owned the world. Which he probably did. Or at least the part of it she was standing on, Rebecca thought ruefully. It was easy to conclude that this was Rosalie's brother. He had the look of her—leashed energy but still a bit untamed. The sun formed a glow around him, making it difficult to see his face under the Stetson. But his body stood out from the landscape behind him like sculpture carved on an ancient temple. To Rebecca he looked like one of the classical Olympic athletes—strength, agility, and grace—but wearing a few more clothes, to her unexpected disappointment. Her eyes widened as she studied his faded blue denim shirt, tucked into equally faded and well-worn jeans, covered by a pair of acorn-colored leather chaps riding low to emphasize his lean hips. He stopped with one foot on the first step, a hand resting on his cocked knee, and looked up at her.

Removing his hat, he grinned. The sun struck gold off the numerous blond streaks running through his tobacco brown hair. "Howdy, ma'am. Are you lost or is there something I can do for you?"

Rebecca held back a chuckle at his greeting. In her line of work she was more used to a salute that ran along the lines of, "Hey mama, how's it goin'?" She met his curious gaze, his eyes light and brilliantly alive. Then the cowboy smiled to reveal perfect teeth, dazzling, achingly white against his tanned skin. It knocked her completely off balance. All she could do was gulp and hope she would make sense when she opened her mouth. No such luck. "You must...I mean..." She extended the bundle in her arms. "Well—here's your baby."

"My baby?" J.D. took a step backward and gaped at her. "I've never seen you before in my life. Have I?" He closed his mouth with a snap and stroked his chin as his eyes narrowed. "No, I would have remembered a woman who looked like you."

Startled by his comment, Rebecca tried to regain her professional calm, the calm she showed to the world so the world wouldn't know how uncertain she felt at times. Taking a deep breath, she stared down at the man who grinned up at her. J.D. tipped his head back, the light shifting to fall directly across his face. He was devastating. That was the only word for it. As if his broad brow, high, chiseled cheekbones and strong jaw weren't enough, his eyes were a clear, beautiful hazel—a light green rimmed with flecks of brown and gold that matched his hair. When those eyes met hers at closer range for the first time, a quiver ran along Rebecca's nerves. She could have sworn she'd just stepped into the air-conditioning.

Struggling to keep her attention on the matter at hand, she said, "Let's start this again. I've come here to see J. D. McCoy—"

"You found him."

"—so I can deliver Rosalie's baby."

J. D. McCoy reeled and clutched the railing as his face drained of all color. "What?"

Gripping the baby more tightly in her arms, Rebecca rushed to the top of stairs. "Mr. McCoy, are you all right?"

He shook his head, like a dog coming out of a stream, and muttered, "Did you say Rosalie's baby? My sister, Rosalie?"

Rebecca took pity on him. "That's right. I'm sorry to blurt it out like that. It was stupid. I'm usually more tactful."

After a long moment, J.D.'s stunned gaze left her face and riveted to the bundle in her arms. Then he came to life.

He bounded up the steps like a mean dog. "Where the hell is she? Is she all right? What did ya do with her?"

Taken aback, Rebecca stuttered, "I…I didn't do anything with her. Not exactly…I told her…but I didn't think…" Rebecca trailed off, and ducked her head as the man opposite her clamped his hands on his narrow hips, obviously getting ready to ask her some more questions she wasn't prepared to answer yet. "Anyway, the last time I saw her she was fine," she concluded in a rush.

"Thank God." His shoulders sagged in relief, before he squared them aggressively a moment later. "But okay or not, when I get my hands on her…"

Rebecca wasn't sure what to say. After all, she was the one who'd encouraged Rosalie to seek out her dreams. Just as she'd wished someone had taken an interest in hers when she was Rosalie's age. But Rebecca didn't expect the girl to take her literally and put things, like her baby, on hold while she did so. She peeked at J. D. McCoy as he paced, trying to keep his emotions leashed, if she was any judge. Rebecca would have to explain, but obviously now was not the time. She had expected him to be upset, since Rosalie had told her they'd parted under some very harsh circumstances. It was a good thing they'd come to an understanding of sorts or Rebecca wouldn't have come here at all.

Finally he stopped muttering and eyed her narrowly. "Why'd she send this baby to me?"

"You're her brother. Besides, if I'd put the paperwork into my agency then the baby would have gone into foster care. Rosalie would have a hard time getting her back after abandoning her…" Rebecca caught herself "…seeming to abandon her."

"Abandoning…" He hesitated. "She—is there something wrong with it?"

"With what?"

Indicating the baby, J.D. backed up, slamming against

the railing bordering the steps. "With the baby. It's not moving."

"She's sleeping. Once she gets to sleep not much wakes this baby." Rebecca snuggled the baby closer and smiled. "Besides, until now, she hasn't slept a wink all day."

Finally, J.D. looked away and murmured, "So, my baby sister has a baby." He was silent for a few moments, his eyes regretful as he pulled his attention back to study the bundle in Rebecca's arms. He reached his hand toward the blanket, but stopped and hooked his thumb into his belt buckle instead. He took a breath, lifting his gaze, obviously steeling himself to ask a series of rapid-fire questions. "So, where's Rosalie. How come you're here with her baby?"

"She left her on my doorstep yesterday morning along with a note directing me here. She said that you'd know what to do."

At that a huge, bitter laugh erupted from J.D. "Hell, that's a joke. I haven't known what to do about *Rosalie* since she was thirteen years old. What makes her think I'll know what to do for her baby?"

Rebecca was quiet as she watched him struggle to understand the situation. "I don't think she meant for you to take care of the baby forever. I'm sure she'll be back very soon."

"Oh, you think so, huh? Well, she didn't come back after she dusted the Texas dirt off her heels three years ago. She made damn sure I couldn't find her, too, no matter how hard I tried. So, what makes you think she's coming back now?"

"She gave me that idea in her note." Rebecca shifted the baby to slide one hand into her pocket and withdraw Rosalie's note. She handed him the torn scrap of paper. "Here, see for yourself."

Gingerly he took it and unfolded it, reading it to himself. After a moment, he folded it carefully. "Mind if I keep this?"

Rebecca shook her head as he tucked it into his jeans pocket. He gnawed on his lower lip for a moment, then reached a hand to draw the blanket away from the sleeping baby. Hesitating, he stepped closer until Rebecca could smell the horses, leather and heat of Texas on the man. Instead of repelling her, she found the scent made her breath come faster. This was a man. A real man, unlike the watered-down versions her society mother kept introducing her to in Boston.

J.D. extended one long finger and gently touched the baby's cheek, looking surprised when the child moved. With a brief smile, he stroked the baby's cheek again. "What's her name?"

"Her name's Jessie." As if she recognized her name, the child stirred. Rebecca glanced up at J.D., surprised to see a shocked look on his face. "What's wrong?"

"Did you say, Jessie?"

"That's right. Rosalie said she named her after someone she loved." The baby stretched and slowly opened her eyes, eyes just beginning to change from blue to something darker.

"Impossible," he said as he stared at the child. "My name's Jesse. Jesse Delaney McCoy. And the last thing my sister said to me was, 'I'll hate you 'til the day I die.'"

Rebecca didn't know what to say for a moment. Suddenly she was suspicious of Rosalie's indication that everything was all right between the two McCoys. Unfortunately there wasn't a thing she could do about changing the situation now. The silence stretched as the baby turned her head and looked at J.D. Then without warning, baby Jessie smiled, a big toothless grin that took them both by surprise. Rebecca chuckled, trying to lighten the mood. "Obviously, her daughter doesn't agree."

J.D. grinned back, he couldn't seem to help it. Babies had a way of making even the grumpy smile. "Well, well, you're gonna to be a charmer, aren't you darlin'."

"She's a very good baby. You won't have any trouble with her."

Holding up his hands, J.D. backed up. "Whoa, hold on there. She can't stay here."

"Well, of course she can stay here. You're her uncle."

"That may be, but I don't know what to do about a baby."

Rebecca sighed as she struggled to hold on to the squirming baby. "I suspected I might have to stay for a few days, to go over the basics. That's my job, helping people learn how to cope with children. That's how I met Rosalie."

"Rosalie came to you for help?"

"No, the social services agency I work for recommended I counsel her."

Just then the baby let out a yell that could be heard in Arizona. J.D. cast a horrified look at Rebecca. "This little one's louder than a corral full of bawling calves."

Uncertainly, Rebecca looked at the baby. As she'd only started working in this capacity with mothers and babies a few months before, when her boss decided she needed a change, Rebecca couldn't understand what was wrong. This baby had never acted like this before. All the way here she'd been as good as gold.

As Jessie continued to squall, Rebecca tore her gaze from the little red face to look up at J. D. McCoy. She had an uneasy feeling that her inexperience was going to show. Hating to show her ineptitude in front of this man, Rebecca tried to glance at her watch. "Maybe she's still hungry."

J.D. strode to the door and held it open. "Come on in then and we'll see what Smoke has going for dinner. Then we can talk about this little problem."

Rebecca hastened into the house, stopping to blink as her eyes adjusted from the bright light outside to the gloom of the hallway. From what she could see she was in a vestibule with a straight staircase rising to the second floor. A saddle was slung over the upper railing along the hallway which looked down into the area where she stood. The table to her right was covered with junk of all types, from ropes to a pair of broken spurs, to a horse bridle and what looked like an old branding iron. As her eyes grew accustomed to the dim light, she became aware of about an inch of dust covering everything in sight, including the pair of antlers mounted on the wall, which J.D. was now using as a hat rack for his Stetson.

"Come on in and make yourself at home, Miss..." He stopped and looked surprised. "I didn't get your name, did I?"

Smiling distractedly as she lifted the squalling baby to her shoulder so she could see her environment, Rebecca said loudly, "You had other things to think about. It's Rebecca Chandler."

"Rebecca," he drawled. She straightened self-consciously as his gaze traveled slowly over her.

Just then Jessie started squirming, forcing Rebecca to rapidly adjust her hold on the child. The way the baby was bending from one side to another, it was like trying to hang on to a Slinky toy. "Could we get to the kitchen, then maybe I can—"

"No problem. It's right down the hall here."

He led the way down the hallway into a wide room that seemed to run the width of the house. At one end was a harvest table and chairs big enough for a family of giants. It was placed appealingly under a window wall that looked out over a garden full of vegetables and flowers. Rebecca's gaze traveled to her right, to the wooden cabinets made of pine planks, open shelves of crockery, and a long expanse of countertop covered with jars, pots and pans, and old tin containers stuffed with scraps of papers that looked like recipes cut from the newspaper. Rebecca frowned. All of these kitchen necessities belonged in cupboards and drawers, not on the countertop. On his way to wash up at the sink, J.D. must have recognized what she was thinking.

"Smoke likes to keep things where he can find them."
Grinning, J.D. indicated the man planted territorially at the
far end of the kitchen. "He says his rheumatism hurts when
he has to bend over."

Patting the baby on the back to quiet her, Rebecca followed his gaze, first seeing a fieldstone fireplace large
enough for a whole steer, then the antique black stove beside it.

There, hunched over a huge pot of smoking *something*
on the stove was a man who looked like he'd just limped
out of an old John Wayne movie. He was wiry, bent and
grizzled, wearing a plaid shirt with holes in the elbows and
tan trousers held up by old-fashioned suspenders. She was
surprised to see him wearing his hat inside. She glanced at
J.D.

"Never takes it off," J.D. murmured, with a wry look.

It was the biggest hat Rebecca had ever seen. Now she
knew what *ten gallon* meant. He'd probably used it to mea-
sure the bubbling concoction in the cauldron.

"Smoke, this here's Rebecca Chandler and she's brought
us Rosalie's baby girl to visit."

"To live, not visit," Rebecca corrected.

Smoke cast one glance over his shoulder then turned, the
concern apparent on his face. "That dang-blamed brat,
Rosalie's okay, ain't she?"

Crossing his arms, J.D. responded, "Rosalie's breathing,
but seems to be among the missing at the moment."

Smoke glanced at Rebecca and the squalling baby.
"That's Rosalie's little girl all right. She makes as much
noise as her mother did."

Jessie was still fussing as she pushed against Rebecca's
shoulder trying to squirm her little body away from her.
Jessie stopped yelling to stick one fist in her mouth, where
she worried it, drooling like a hungry puppy.

Smoke waved toward the table. "Sit yourself down,

missy, my Texas red stew will stop that caterwauling. See if it don't.''

"Stew? I don't think she's ready for that," Rebecca croaked as she watched the man ladle something that looked like lumpy mud into a bowl. Although she had to admit it smelled delicious—spicy and as rough and sharp as Smoke's conversation, she'd bet.

"Hey, Reb. Maybe she needs a bottle or something," J.D. suggested.

"Rebecca," she said, automatically correcting him.

Scratching his head, J.D. looked around the kitchen. He snapped his fingers, sent Smoke a sideways look and grinned. "I've got a bottle I use to feed abandoned calves. That would work, I guess."

"Good God, how can you—" Then Rebecca stared at him, caught by the tremor at the edge of his mouth. Feeling a fool, she made a face. "Oh. You're joking, aren't you?" However, he now met her gaze with such an innocent expression that she wasn't sure. Except there was a little twinkle lurking, inviting her to grin, which she resisted. She sent him a stern glare instead. After all, babies were serious business. Especially when you didn't really know what you were doing. Rebecca had already discovered when it came to babies, book learning was one thing—reality was another! Not for the first time, she wondered why she'd gotten mixed up with this situation.

Rebecca rocked in place for a moment, trying to settle Jessie, then she grasped at the only solution she could think of. "I have her baby bag in the car, with some formula and a bottle inside. If you'll hold her, I'll go get it." With two quick steps in J.D.'s direction she thrust the baby into his stiff arms as he backed up against the kitchen cabinets to try to avoid her. Then she whirled around to race out to the car.

Rebecca dashed down the steps. *J.D. wouldn't really consider feeding Jessie with a calf's bottle, would he?* Then she told herself to stop being such an idiot. Just because she was out of her depth didn't mean she had to behave like a complete greenhorn. He was kidding, of course. Lord, she had to learn to lighten up. Running across the gravel driveway, she acknowledged that had been a problem most of her life. She was always searching for the serious side and forgetting that often the line between tragedy and comedy was very thin indeed.

Opening the back door of the car, she reached inside and found the plastic baby bag she had given Rosalie. She unzipped it, flipped the cover back and plunged her hands inside, scrambling around to be certain she had put the extra empty bottle and formula there and not accidentally into the trunk. There they were, right next to the box of cereal and a jar of baby peaches she'd fed the baby earlier. Holding the bottle, she sank back onto the seat and stared at the ranch house. All her previous doubts came rushing back. Not just about her own suitability for the direction her career was taking, but also about her wisdom in taking this child to her uncle.

"What am I doing? How can I walk away in a few days and leave this baby?"

During their last session, Rosalie had implied that her brother knew all about the child…had even been expecting them to come for a visit. Obviously that wasn't the case. If Rebecca had known that she would never have impulsively taken this trip. She felt betrayed. She knew she should have put the baby into the social service system immediately. But she couldn't. She had such a strong feeling that Rosalie wanted nothing more than to be a good mother and really be there for Jessie, regardless of the circumstances. So, she couldn't do it. Rebecca imagined herself in the same situation. She had seen too many broken families, including her own. She wanted this young mother and her baby to have a chance—a chance to be part of a family. Now she wondered if she had been totally out of her mind. If her boss found out about it, she could be out of a job as well. He was a stickler for the rules.

Rebecca could still hear Jessie's muted crying competing with the trill of the evening birds and the buzzing insects. She was aware of the sounds of nature here in a way she'd never paid attention to before. She wondered what else she hadn't noticed. She slanted a glance toward the sun dropping low to meet the horizon, seeming to almost touch the hilltop where a stand of trees kept watch against the encroaching prairie. Rebecca felt some of the calm of the day's end seep into her. There was a peace, an inevitability to life here, that she'd never felt in Boston.

It felt good. She inhaled the hot, clean air. Thinking hard, Rebecca glanced back at the house and thought of her first glimpse of Smoke and her last glance of Jessie in J.D.'s arms. Could she trust the Wild West duo inside not to feed the kid to the cows or something? Probably not! Not that she was a whole lot better. She wasn't the most experienced baby handler yet, so she wasn't sure she'd be any better for Jessie full-time than her uncle would be.

Rebecca gnawed on her lower lip. She wasn't sure what to do, which was unusual for her. She prided herself on her competence. At least she *had* until her boss had forced her to accept this type of intimate family interaction role, instead of the aggressive courtroom advocate role she was used to playing. But her ineptitude didn't matter. Because of her actions, Rebecca now felt responsible for Jessie's well-being and she took her obligations very much to heart. That's what came of being the only child of a parent who shrugged off responsibilities as easily as she did husbands.

Rebecca studied the baby items clenched in her hands. She had two weeks of vacation. Surely Rosalie would show up by that time. With a decisive nod, Rebecca repacked the diaper bag, slung it over her shoulder and walked quickly to the house to rescue J. D. McCoy.

2

J.D. held the crying baby at arm's length. He'd tried to hold her closer but in her distress her arms and legs were outstretched and her spine was ramrod straight. It was like holding on to a tree branch. Since he was afraid he might break her or something, he extended his arms and suspended her in space.

"What do you think's the matter with her, Smoke?"

"Beats me." With one finger, Smoke pushed up the brim of his hat. "Got a good set of lungs though, don't she?"

J.D. winced as a particularly high-pitched squeal pierced his eardrum. "It's the McCoy temper, I reckon."

Smoke chuckled. "Well, if she's got you and your sister's blood, can't help it can she?"

"Guess not. No, I guess none of us McCoys can help it. After all, it was my own temper that sent Rosalie away."

Ladling more stew into bowls, Smoke looked over his shoulder. "You ain't the cause of that ornery sister of yours runnin' away. She decided that herself."

"I know, but still I should have…" He trailed off, hating to admit he'd made a big mistake handling his sister. If he hadn't fought with her that evening three years ago, she might still be here safe and sound where she belonged. Instead she'd kept on the move, hiding herself so well, he'd been unable to find her. Every night that had eaten at him, filled him with a sense of failure that he'd found hard to stomach.

"I told ya and told ya, boy. Guilt is a waste of time."

J.D. sent him a brief grin and attempted to pull Rosalie's baby a bit closer. As she started to kick, he changed his mind.

God, what am I going to do with a baby? I can't keep her here. It's impossible. He had enough to do worrying about his stock without worrying about a baby. He glanced at Smoke. No hope there. Smoke would deny it until he was out of breath, but he was not up to it, either—not on a full-time basis. And J.D. didn't expect his sister to happily return to her childhood home, regardless of what Rebecca thought. Rosalie had been too miserable here after their mom died. He stared at the infant, who was still raging like a mini-tornado.

No, it would be much better for the baby if she had a proper home. His heart twisted. It wasn't that he didn't want her, but his history of dealing with most of the women in his life wasn't too great. So, he didn't have much hope with Jessie. J.D. was determined not to mess up another McCoy's life. He'd have to tell Rebecca Chandler when she got back. Once again J.D. attempted to draw his niece close, to try to apologize for what he would be forced to do. Jessie's angry red face and flailing arms changed his mind. He extended his arms as before, trying to wait it out, like he would with a horse that needed breaking. He was sure relieved when Rebecca walked back into the kitchen.

Swinging around in Rebecca's direction, J.D. pleaded, "Here, Reb, take her before she busts something."

"Like my eardrums," Smoke added.

"Oh, no." Placing her bag on the table, she bustled over to J.D. "That's not the way to hold her. You need to give her some comfort, not treat her like a block of concrete." She tried to encourage him to bend his arms and pull the baby closer. "Talk to her softly."

"Softly." J.D.'s eyebrows lifted until they almost disappeared under the shock of hair falling onto his forehead. "I can scarcely hear myself over her when she decides to let loose."

Smoke grinned as he limped past them to place the bowls of stew on the table. "You listen to the lady now, boy."

"And cuddle her." Rebecca mimed pulling the baby close to her chest.

"She's kicking like a just-roped calf. You cuddle her." J.D. held Jessie out to Rebecca, but she avoided taking her. She reached around to rub the baby's back.

"You're doing fine."

Chuckling, Smoke added his two cents. "Pretend she's one of your favorite cows, J.D. Remember that time I found you in the stable when you were just a brat-faced kid?"

J.D. frowned. "Shut up, Smoke." It had no effect, which wasn't a surprise. Smoke had known him since he was a baby.

"You'd got into your pa's liquor and were so lit up you lay right down in the straw and kissed a cow."

With the baby now relaxing a bit, Rebecca continued to rub her back and urge her into J.D.'s arms. Wrinkling her nose, she asked, "Did you really kiss a cow?"

"I like cows. They have the most beautiful big, round brown eyes," he said, a smile twitching at the corner of his mouth. He took a close look at her as she pressed against his side, urging the baby closer into his arms. "Sort of like yours."

"My eyes aren't brown."

"No, but they're big and round and expressive as hell."

J.D. flushed. What was the matter with him? He was standing here with an unhappy baby babbling about cows and Rebecca's big blue eyes. He scowled. This woman had completely upset his routine and he didn't like it. He turned quickly and thrust Jessie into Rebecca's arms. He stepped away to put some distance between them.

J.D. liked his routine. He liked coming in at night after a hard day on the range and not having to bother with anyone. He liked eating whatever Smoke felt like making that day. He liked showering and doing what he pleased for the rest of the evening. Sometimes he did paperwork at his desk. Sometimes he read or stretched out in his favorite chair in the den and watched TV. But whatever he did, it was *his* routine. He glanced at the woman and baby who had taken over his kitchen. If he didn't speak up, he had a feeling all that could be history. And if there was one thing he knew about history—it repeated itself. His particular history wasn't something he ever wanted to live through again. It had damn near killed him the first time.

Uncertainly he glanced at Jessie who had calmed down and now rested her head against Rebecca's shoulder. *Lord, she was a cute little thing.* She had funny little ears, with the slightest suggestion of a point…just like his sister.

Oh, damn.

He didn't want to be responsible for a baby, any baby. But this was his sister's child, his niece. What would happen if he refused to take her? Could he refuse? Feeling caught in a trap, he stalked over to the table and pulled out a chair, attempting to avoid the subject for a while longer. He indicated the seat. "You might as well sit down and have some dinner since Smoke has it ready." He hesitated and looked over at Rebecca and the child. "Unless you want to feed the baby first. Although she seems to have quieted down."

"Yes, she has. But I think I'll make a bottle for her anyway."

Smoke bobbed up from the table. "I'll do that missy, you just set a spell."

"That's okay, I can handle it. We might as well have Jessie get used to being around her uncle." With that she marched over and placed the baby in J.D.'s arms again.

"Uh, I don't think…"

"You have to get to know her. Babies this age start knowing where they belong, and Jessie belongs here."

"No, Jessie belongs with her mother." He tried to keep the anger and the built-up hurt out of his voice. If this stunt wasn't just like Rosalie, he didn't know what was. She was always leaving him to deal with her mess.

Rebecca balled her fists on her hips. "I know, but right now that isn't possible, so you're it."

He bristled at her bossy tone. She reminded him of his fifth-grade teacher. "No. I'm not. I can't take care of a baby, I need to be out running the ranch during the daytime, not in here baby-sitting." Then to avoid Rebecca's accusing eyes, and feeling sudden guilt at his reluctance, J.D. looked at the old man at the other end of the table, blurting, "Smoke what if—"

"Nope. Not if you're meaning what I think you're meaning." Smoke leaned back in his chair and folded his hands over his full stomach. "It ain't a good idea."

"It might work. You don't have to ride the range anymore." Desperately J.D. tried to convince himself that it could be a solution, even though he knew better.

Smoke drew himself up with dignity. "I got other things to do, boy. Do you think them vegetables out there take care of themselves? Then there's the cooking, and the picking up after everybody."

With the ease of long habit, J.D. fell into arguing-with-Smoke mode. "What everybody? You and I are the only ones here."

"Tain't so. There's Clint and Roy."

"Clint goes home to his wife every night, and Roy takes care of himself out there in the bunkhouse. Your cooking gives him indigestion."

"Please, stop." Rebecca broke into this exchange with an exasperated snort. "Look, J.D., you might as well face facts. Rosalie asked me to bring this baby to you and I did.

She shouldn't have left her—I shouldn't have taken her! But I did. Unfortunately, we'll have to deal with it.''

J.D. eyed Rebecca. "Then you might have to stick around a bit longer than you'd planned, Miss Chandler.'' The minute the words popped out, he started wondering if he was totally insane to suggest it. If there was one thing he didn't need it was a woman around cluttering up the place. Unfortunately he could see no way around it. He slid her a peek under his lashes. At least she was decorative.

"I already thought of that. I'm completely prepared to stay here until Rosalie comes back.''

Suddenly amused by her determined tone, he couldn't help adding, "You realize you could have quite a wait out here in the middle of nowhere, don't you?''

Rebecca shrugged his comment off as if it weren't worth listening to. The only reason he saw the faint shadow of doubt cloud her eyes for a moment was because he was watching her closely for a reaction. "I just started two weeks' vacation and I'd planned to experience Texas anyway. This is as good a way as any. As of now, my vacation will be here, with Jessie.''

All of a sudden, J.D. felt uncomfortable. What the hell was he doing? What if he got used to having her around. "Maybe I shouldn't have sugg—''

"Too late.'' She folded her arms, delivering an ultimatum. "Look, you have two choices. Either I stay and you put up with me and the baby. Or I go and leave the baby alone with you. Would you like to think about it?''

Realizing he'd just paint himself into a corner either way he answered, J.D. did the smart thing and kept his mouth shut as Rebecca smiled down at him. He gritted his teeth. She wore that patient, amused smile women use when they know they have you right where they want you. When he didn't respond, she snatched the diaper bag from the table, turned on her heel and marched to the sink.

J.D. watched Rebecca as she dipped her hand inside the

bag, then withdrew a can of formula and started to prepare the bottle. Then he tore his gaze away to look down at the bundle in his arms, who was chewing on her fist and making noises. "Hey there, Jessie," he whispered, surprised when she shifted her attention from her knuckles to him. Her eyes widened. She looked at him and managed to get her thumb into her mouth. Making little smacking noises, Jessie sucked hard as she watched him. Encouraged, J.D. tried again. "Hey, there."

With a stealthy finger he stroked her skin, amazed at how soft it was, like the downy fuzz of one of the baby chicks in his henhouse. "So, what do you think so far?" He lifted her other hand and studied her long fingers. They were so perfect, so tiny and perfect. He hadn't realized they'd be like that. He felt a sharp ache. *If things had been different, I would have had a child of my own by now.* The thought astonished him. Then Jessie finished the job by closing her fingers around his in a tight grip, hanging on as if she knew what he was thinking.

He peered at her face. Jessie did have the look of her mother. There was a suggestion of Rosalie's eyebrows and the shape of her face. He remembered his sister as a child. She'd been so sweet and loving. It was only later she'd become such a handful. J.D. shifted abruptly as he remembered how angry he still was at his sister for putting him through hell for the past few years. He moved so abruptly that the baby jerked and let out a small yell.

"Whoops. Sorry 'bout that, sweetheart."

Wishing Rebecca would hurry, J.D. glanced up to watch her pour the formula into the baby bottle. Watching her spill some on the counter, he realized she didn't look quite as competent with the procedure as he'd expected. That made him feel better for some reason. Smiling down at his niece he murmured, "Dinner's on its way, darlin'."

"That's right," Smoke commented with a grin, "you sweet-talk her. Females love that."

J.D. chuckled. "Now, how would you know that? The only female you every had any tolerance for was your horse."

"Well, that's not your problem, boy. Your problem is getting rid of all the women who're chasing you." Smoke chortled, indicated Rebecca and whispered, "Now, that one…something tells me that one is in a different league altogether."

J.D. looked across the kitchen to the slim figure of Rebecca, who was testing the temperature of the bottle. He had a funny feeling Smoke was right. Getting used to a baby around was bad enough, but the sight of Rebecca Chandler every day might prove downright hazardous to his peace of mind. She was way too attractive—and way too determined. Before he knew it, this woman would have him powdering baby bottoms and changing diapers. With every pore, J.D. absorbed the way she moved as she sauntered back toward him across the kitchen, all curving hips and long legs. It stirred his imagination, with other parts of his body not far behind.

Rebecca handed him the bottle. "Here. This is one of the first things you have to learn."

Is she serious? J.D. considered her. Yep, looked like it from the way her lips had firmed into a no-nonsense line. He almost smiled. After all, he knew what to do with a bottle. He'd been feeding orphaned animals since he was a boy. But if he did it, this little city gal would expect him to follow her lead from now on. J.D. didn't like that idea. He was generally the one doing the leading. He didn't respond well to some filly, no matter how tempting, trying to put a bridle on him before he was ready.

He tried to hand the bottle back. "I don't think this is a good idea."

"Sure it is." Rebecca slanted a look from him to Smoke who was chortling into his stew. Then she arched an elegant eyebrow, smiled and placed her hand over his to lift the bottle to Jessie's lips. "Now, you just pretend she's a calf, J.D. Put that nipple into her mouth and hang on."

Rebecca watched as Jessie latched on and sucked hard at the bottle. Then, to her surprise, the baby pushed it away and let out a single howl. For a moment, Rebecca was as confused as J.D., until she saw the baby starting to bump her mouth with her fist and drool once again. Inspiration hit. "Maybe she's cutting a tooth!"

Eyebrows lifting, J.D. considered Jessie. "Isn't she too little to have teeth?"

"I don't think so."

"You don't think so? I thought you were the expert?"

The tip of her nose turned bright pink. "I wouldn't use the word *expert* exactly."

J.D. had to stop his lips from twitching as she tried to button herself back into her authoritative self. "What would you call your—"

"You see, every baby is different. Jessie's almost six months, but I've read the first teeth can come anywhere from four months on."

J.D. grinned at Smoke, shoveling in the last of his stew. "There you see Smoke, you still have hope." He pretended to duck when Smoke threatened him with his upraised spoon.

"My teeth are just fine, boy. When I need 'em, I stick 'em in."

"I know." Chuckling, J.D. nodded at him. "But I didn't pay that big dentist bill so you can carry them around in your shirt pocket most of the day, old man."

"Well, the dang-blamed things aren't something you just up and get used to, ya know."

Rebecca almost winced when J.D. displayed his perfect teeth in a wide smile at Smoke's comment. At first she was surprised J.D. would mention something so personal in front of a stranger. But this was obviously an old bone between the two of them, and one they thoroughly enjoyed wrangling about. It seemed an odd thing to joke about, she thought, but perhaps Texans had a different sense of humor than easterners.

"Uh, J.D...." Afraid she'd succumb to her curiosity and ask Smoke how he could eat with no teeth if the conversation continued, Rebecca changed the subject. "Stick your finger in Jessie's mouth and tell me if you feel anything."

"No way." He started to lift the baby to hand her to Rebecca. "You do it."

Rebecca gave him a wide-eyed glance, saying in a sweet tone calculated to get a response. "You're not afraid of her are you?"

"Not at all," J.D. replied with aplomb. "I haven't washed up yet is all. I don't want to give her germs."

Treating him like a prize student, Rebecca beamed. "Oh, I'm proud of you. That's good thinking."

"Gee, thanks, teach. Glad you approve."

Rebecca lifted her brows at him then walked over and washed her hands, saying over her shoulder. "I'll try instead." Marching back to J.D.'s side, she bent over to run a finger over Jessie's gums. The baby flinched and closed her mouth. Rebecca was so close to J.D. that her hair brushed his cheek. Once again she became aware of how overwhelmingly masculine he was. "Uh, nothing's breaking through, but the bottom gum feels a bit swollen right in the front. Sometimes if you rub it a bit, it takes some of the hurt away."

She proceeded to add action to words, then almost jumped a foot when J.D. tucked a lock of hair that had swung forward behind her ears.

"That's my philosophy, too." There was a smile in his voice that disconcerted Rebecca even more.

"Try...try... maybe she'll take some milk now. I fed her shortly after the plane landed so she shouldn't need anything else tonight but this bottle." She made the mistake of glancing to her left. Her eyes met his twinkling gaze.

She jerked her attention back to Jessie, withdrew her finger and straightened. "If we can get her to drink it."

"I'll give it a shot." With an awkward movement J.D. shifted the baby as he crossed his foot over his knee, creating a nice little cradle for the baby to lie in. Hesitantly he offered the nipple to the baby, and grinned when she clamped down on it. "Just like a female...changed her mind already."

Rebecca raised a haughty eyebrow. "Pardon?"

A laugh exploded from Smoke as he stood to pat his pockets. "If I was you, J.D., I'd watch my tongue from now on."

J.D. peeked up at Rebecca saying in a teasing tone, "I was talking about females in general, you understand. I'm sure you're much too sensible to run around acting irrationally and changing your mind every minute."

Rebecca looked away. *That's what he thought.* Coming here had been the most irrational act of her life. What if she was wrong and Rosalie didn't come back? Could she convince J. D. McCoy to accept responsibility for his niece, or would the baby be better off with an adopted family? After all, many childless couples were hungering for babies. Since it was too soon to put any of these thoughts into words, she ignored his comment. Instead, she concentrated on Smoke as he withdrew a pack of tobacco and a roll of cigarette papers.

"I don't mean to be rude, but please don't smoke around the baby. It's not good for her." She hoped she didn't sound prim, but at the look Smoke sent her, she was sure she did. Rebecca stood her ground. She was responsible for this baby's health.

Smoke flushed red under his scraggly white whiskers. Disconcerted, he put his pouch back in his pocket. "Well, I'll be... Now looky here, I been on this ranch for nigh on forty years. You been here for about fifteen minutes. To my way of thinkin', if I want to suck a puff after dinner—"

"Smoke," J.D. said quietly, as he lifted his gaze from Jessie, "she's right. Take it outside, okay?"

With one sheepish look at his boss, Smoke ambled toward the door and pushed his way outside, muttering under his breath all the way.

Except for the gulping sounds of the avidly sucking baby, the kitchen was silent. Rebecca had never heard such silence. It was terrifying. She peeked at J.D., suddenly needing to make contact. "I didn't mean to cause trouble...."

"Don't worry about it. He'll get over it. His bark's worse than his bite."

For a moment a pain crept into her heart as she watched J. D. McCoy and Jessie. The scene in the kitchen looked and felt so right to her...so homey. There was something about a big, tough male cradling an infant that went straight to her dreams. Dreams she kept hidden, even from herself. She blinked rapidly, then forced herself to study the situation analytically.

Even though J.D. looked uncomfortable, Rebecca could imagine the time when he would handle this baby with the ease that he probably handled his horse—or his woman. Rebecca had no idea where that last thought had come from. Although she did seem to remember Rosalie talking about the women always hanging around being nice to her so they could get to J.D. more easily.

"Sit down and eat your stew, Reb. Smoke makes great stew."

"Rebecca," she corrected. Anxious to find something to do with her hands so she wouldn't be tempted to plunge them into his tousled hair, she walked around the table to sit down. Picking up her spoon she dug into the stew and absently took a big bite. At the spicy taste she gasped, coughed and reached for the pitcher of water Smoke had placed on the table earlier. She poured herself a glass and took a big gulp. "Wow."

J.D. chuckled. "Don't worry, you'll get used to it. Try another bite."

She did and found to her surprise that the second bite went down easier and so did the others. Before she knew it she was scraping the bowl clean. "What's in this?"

"Haven't a clue. Smoke's been guarding the recipe for that stew since he used to cook it over a campfire when I was a kid."

"Maybe I can ask him in a weak moment."

"Smoke doesn't have too many weak moments. Especially since you've sent him and his beloved butts outside."

Rebecca shifted uncomfortably. "You did that, remember? I only suggested it first."

Hesitantly J.D. fingered Jessie's wispy curls. "Well, it was the right thing to do."

"And you always do the right thing?" In her experience, such uncompromising honor was rare.

J.D. sent her a long, thoughtful look. "Nope...not always. Sometimes I bend over backward to do the very thing that's gonna get me in big trouble."

Curious, but not sure how to respond to that, Rebecca looked away from him and concentrated on Jessie who had almost drained her bottle of formula. Satisfied, Rebecca leaned back in her chair and indicated the baby. "I'll take her now, if you'd like."

"Good idea. I have to find somewhere for you to sleep."

"Where do you suggest?"

He controlled the quirk of his lips, before saying with a deadpan expression, "A couple of ideas do come to mind Re...bec...ca."

Rebecca felt the color rush into her cheeks, at the sexy way he drew out her name. It gave her images she'd be better off not thinking about. "I know you're just teasing, but that type of thing is not the best idea. What if I took you seriously?"

"Well," J.D. drawled, "that might be interesting."

God knew she was tempted! She was surprised at how tempted. It put her hackles up. "I don't think so. I'm here because of Rosalie and the baby. I have no intention of becoming a plaything for some male's overactive—"

Eyes twinkling, he stood up, leaned over and plunked the baby into her waving arms. "Shhh…calm down, Reb. I was just joking. Seeing how fast you'd rise to the bait. It's a bad habit of mine."

"Rebecca."

"Yes, ma'am." He practically threw her a salute. "Tell you what, I'm going upstairs to see about sleeping arrangements. Y'all come on up when you're finished down here."

Relieved, Rebecca watched him saunter from the room. She lifted Jessie over her shoulder and unthinkingly patted her back. Jessie let out a big burp and promptly spit up all over Rebecca's shoulder. "Oh, no!" She got to her feet and marched to the sink. Shifting the baby into the crook of one arm, she wet a paper towel, wiped the baby's chin and with another damp towel, scrubbed the nubby, silk fabric of her suit. After throwing both towels away, she dashed a hand across her burning eyes. It had been quite a day. She felt as if she'd walked into another world since leaving Boston early this morning.

"Girl," she said to her reflection in the window, "you need about eight hours sleep and then you'll be able to handle J. D. McCoy, or any other damn cowboy who gets in your way."

Rebecca picked up the diaper bag and slung it over her shoulder before turning and leaving the kitchen. She headed for the stairs. As she climbed the steps to find J.D.'s promised bedroom, she realized Jessie was beginning to nod off to sleep. She jiggled her to keep her awake. "Don't you go to sleep now little one, or you'll be up all night. And so will I." At the top of the stairs she stopped and looked left, noticing the saddle which still rode the banister waiting only for its rider. She thought the saddle an odd sort of decoration. Then she remembered the bridle on the table downstairs and decided the horse was probably misplaced instead. Rebecca inhaled and set her chin into its battle stance. *Someone needs to take control here.* Although she was usually very good at restoring order, she had a feeling that getting control of the house was probably easier than trying to get control of its owner.

She peered down the dim hallway, illuminated only by the last remnants of the summer light. Looking for J.D., she turned left and peeked into a door opening off the hallway. She got a quick glimpse of a large room with an old-fashioned poster bed. The master bedroom, she guessed. Then she heard some thumping sounds and turned around. "J.D.?"

"Down the hall."

She jiggled Jessie again, relieved to see her eyes pop open, and walked toward his voice. Expecting to see J.D., Rebecca opened a closed door. A peek inside showed her an unused room with a bare bed piled high with boxes. She wondered if it was Rosalie's old room. Rebecca hoped with all her heart Rosalie would show up to sleep in it again. She pulled the door shut and after calling his name again, finally located J.D. in a small room at the end of the passage. He was competently tucking in the top sheet on a long, narrow bed tucked against one side of the room and nestled cozily under a window. He glanced over his shoulder. "I know it's kind of small, but—"

"It's fine, thanks." Rebecca looked around, noticing the trophies on the shelf over the student-sized desk, along with the old family pictures, high school letters and ribbons which were framed and mounted on the wall. This room screamed of belonging, of permanence, of family history and tradition. She envied that.

"Is this your room?"

"Was, when I was a boy. Now, I sleep in the master

bedroom.'' J.D. straightened up and indicated the bed. ''Bit too narrow for my taste.''

Rebecca glanced at his impressive shoulders and chest, her eyes continuing down his long, rangy body. She tried to lose the sudden image of J.D. stretched out on that bed. Licking her dry lips, she said, ''I'm sure it is.''

''I thought you and the baby could sleep in here tonight. Tomorrow I can rearrange things and get into the attic to find the baby bed.''

''You have a baby bed?''

J.D. grinned. ''Well sure, what'd you think? My sister and I were bedded down in the barn?''

''What I mean was…many times people give them away after the children outgrow them.''

Shaking his head, J.D. grabbed a lightweight quilt and spread it over the bed. ''Not my family. We keep everything.''

Looking around, Rebecca asked, ''Where should I put the baby tonight?''

''I thought we could get some bales of hay and bed her down on the floor between them.''

Rebecca gasped. ''You wouldn't…''

Amused, J.D. slapped his knee. ''Reb, honest, you are the most gullible little thing.''

At five foot seven, Rebecca couldn't remember the last time someone had called her little. Of course, to someone six-two or more, she supposed anyone would look small. However, she refused to take any more bait, asking in a precise tone. ''Where do you suggest we put this child for the evening?''

Chuckling, J.D. leaned over and pulled a trundle bed from under the narrow one. ''I think it might work for Jessie tonight, don't you?''

Relieved, Rebecca studied the bed, which was only about a foot off the floor. ''I think so…especially if we put some pillows around her. She isn't crawling yet so she can't move very far.''

J.D. squeezed past her to reach the closet. ''I'll get another sheet and blanket.'' Opening the door, he removed some bedding from the top shelf then turned to Rebecca. His gaze sharpened as it skimmed over her face. He indicated the desk chair across the room. ''Why don't you sit down over there. You look exhausted. The heat can take a lot out of you if you're not used to it.''

Climbing over the bed, Rebecca did as he suggested. Sighing, she sat on the chair and turned Jessie to sit on her lap facing her uncle. Jessie started to coo and gurgle as they watched J.D. stretch and bend to make the bed.

J.D. glanced at the baby. ''She sounds a bit happier.''

''Probably because she just spit up all over me.''

Grinning, J.D. met her gaze. ''That's what that smell is, eh? I didn't think it was perfume.''

''Eau de sour milk?'' Unable to resist his grin, Rebecca grinned back. ''Do you think there's a market for it?''

He hooked his thumbs in his belt. ''From what I remember of her attitude, my sister sure wouldn't have bought it. She had other plans.''

Rebecca dropped a kiss on Jessie's head before she answered. ''What you plan doesn't always work out.''

He slid the trundle bed halfway under the bed so he could sit on the top one. ''I know all about that one.''

''Me, too.'' She lifted her gaze, to find his intriguing eyes focused on hers.

''You do? That's a surprise. You look like the kind of woman who makes sure everything goes exactly the way it's meant to be.''

He should only know! Lately the independent career woman seemed to be taking a back seat to the part of her that needed to be needed. However, with her bad luck at relationships, that side wasn't doing very well, either.

Rebecca tightened her grip on the baby. Crossing her leg,

she nervously bounced Jessie on a pretend horsey ride.
There was something about the intensity of this man's gaze
that sent her thoughts scattering in disturbing directions.
"I… think every woman should follow her own destiny."

J.D. crossed his ankle over his knee and leaned forward.
"What if that destiny leads a woman where she shouldn't
be?"

"I believe, she still has to follow it until she figures it
out for herself." Wasn't this what she'd been doing lately?
She sure hoped so.

"No matter who she hurts in the process?"

Rebecca hesitated, unsure if he was just making conversation. Was he speaking of his sister or perhaps…another
personal situation? She didn't care for that last idea. Cautiously, she asked, "Are you speaking hypothetically?"

He stared at her for a long moment. He rubbed his palms
on his knees as his lips twisted into a rather grim smile.
"Yeah, hypothetically. Just seeing if I could get another
rise out of you." He unfolded from the bed, rising to his
full height. He walked to the door, but stopped to stretch a
hand on the doorjamb. "Where are your keys? I'll get your
luggage and bring it up."

"They're in my purse. I left it on the table downstairs."

"Don't worry. I'll bring that up, too." With that he
stepped into the hallway.

"J.D.?" She gulped as he turned with the fluid motion
of a mountain lion. "I'd like to take a shower before bed.
Would that be all right?"

His brow lifted and he suddenly seemed to have problems keeping his lips from twitching. "Are you asking for
my opinion…or my help?" A gleam of unholy amusement
lightened his expression, as if the tension and surprise of
their arrival had been too much and the emotion needed
somewhere to go.

She rolled her eyes at his outrageous expression. "What
I meant was…is it okay water-wise for me to do that?"

Thoughtfully, he scraped his knuckles over his late-day beard stubble. "We do have inside plumbing, you know. You washed your hands right down there in the kitchen sink. Remember?"

"That wasn't what I meant." She stood up, placing one hand under the baby's bottom so the babbling baby still faced J.D. "I know it's often dry in Texas. I've read about cisterns and what happens when the water gets low, so I could come up with a schedule that would—" She jerked to a stop, sure he was laughing at her. "Oh, never mind. Where's the bathroom?"

J.D. kept his expression polite and pointed. "Other end of the hall."

With a brief thanks she strode to the bed to place Jessie on the faded quilt. *Would she never stop trying to make over the world to suit her point of view?*

"Reb?"

"For the last time. Don't call me Reb."

"'Scuse me, sugar, it slipped out."

She glared over her shoulder. "Don't call me sugar, either."

He dipped his head to stare at the floor. "Yes, ma'am. No offense ma'am, only…"

She wasn't having any of his humble act. "What?"

"Regarding your questions about cisterns…ma'am." Smiling he added, "They were mighty smart questions, and I appreciate you thinking about our circumstances."

Rebecca pursed her lips, waiting for the other shoe to drop. J. D. McCoy looked like a boy intent on mischief. And what better target than a visitor from what might as well be another world? She had a feeling his teasing must have driven the teenage Rosalie nuts. Rebecca hoped she'd survive it.

"However, to set your mind at ease, we've had a wetter spring than usual. Plus, we have a freshwater well so you don't have to worry too much about not being shiny clean while you're here.'' He sent her a swift grin. ''Besides, to this here country boy, you'd still look mighty good mussed up a bit.''

She stopped herself from responding when she got a good look at the vibrant twinkle in his eyes. *Country boy, my foot! More charm than the devil is more accurate.* She had to work hard not to succumb to his lighthearted expression. Drawing her customary authority around her she inclined her head, graciously she hoped. Although she was tempted to box his ears for him and show him what city women were made of, she controlled her impulse, saying instead, ''Perhaps you could also bring in the baby seat that's in the back of the car, as well as our luggage.''

He straightened from his casual stance by the doorway. ''Consider it done…ma'am.''

As she watched him disappear down the hall, she wondered why the word *ma'am* had made her shiver. Was it because it sounded like a caress when spoken by his deep, drawling voice? She looked down at Jessie, who was lying happily on the bed trying to remove her socks to find her toes. ''So, what do you think of your uncle?''

The baby paused, giving her a round-eyed look. Finally she took a deep breath, arched her back, puckered up and uttered a loud, ''Ooohhh!''

Rebecca looked back at the doorway, through which one of the hottest males she'd ever met in her entire life had just disappeared.

''I couldn't have said it better myself.''

3

————→←————

About two o'clock in the morning, Jessie's fussing yanked Rebecca from her fitful sleep. Rebecca never slept well in strange beds, anyway. But when you added in Smoke's spicy stew and the way her stomach was still boiling, she was amazed she'd slept at all. Blinking in the moonlight as Jessie's whimpers crept into her consciousness, Rebecca reached down a hand to pat the restless baby.

"Shhh. It's all right, Jessie."

For a moment she wondered if Jessie had indigestion, too; but then she awakened enough to realize it was probably her sore mouth instead. "I'll have to find something to help, sweetheart."

Where was she going to find that, she wondered. Her eyes practically crossed as she tried to concentrate. She wasn't at her best without her usual quotient of sleep. Knowing she had no remedies in her bag, she remembered someone telling her about a medicine that could numb the pain of tender gums.

There was no help for it. She'd have to go raid J. D. McCoy's medicine cabinet and hope for the best.

As she moved to the end of the bed, a clenching pain in her midsection made Rebecca wonder if whatever she found for Jessie's mouth would work for her churning stomach, too. Easing herself to the floor, she stooped to rearrange the pillows around the baby. As she smoothed the restless child's hair, she promised, "I'll be right back and make it all better."

She hesitated, wondering whether to look for a robe in her bag, then decided against it. Nobody would be awake this time of night. Ranch people had to get up early. Another little whimper from Jessie sent Rebecca straight for the door. She slipped into the dimly lit, deserted hallway and tiptoed down the worn carpet runner toward the bathroom. She'd just passed the master bedroom door when a voice behind her made her jump.

"Did I hear a baby crying?"

With the low cry of a trapped animal, Rebecca whirled around and slammed back against the wall. She stared at J. D. McCoy as he stood just outside his bedroom door wearing a partially buttoned pair of jeans and nothing else. A different sort of shiver raced over her nerves as she took in his broad chest, sculpted muscles and endearingly mussed hair.

"You practically made me jump out of my skin."

J.D.'s glance raced over the appealing woman plastered against his wallpaper. "Now, that would be a pity." Right then and there he decided that her skin was probably way too smooth and inviting to a man's touch to be left on the floor of his upstairs hall.

"I didn't mean to scare you. I thought I heard Jessie crying or something."

Still breathing like a long-distance runner, Rebecca's wide eyes met his. She licked her lips before saying, "You did."

"Thought so." J.D. wanted to say more but he was caught by the way her nightclothes draped over her curvy form. Of course, he was also caught by the fact that her sleeping attire was entirely unexpected.

"I would have thought you the type for silk, not a ratty old Boston College T-shirt."

Warm color swept over her cheeks, the rose tint making

her eyes look bluer than ever. "That sounded just like my mother."

J.D.'s eyebrows lifted, his gaze lingering on the delicate curve of her neck as it rose from the round neckline. Ratty old cotton or not, the material still hugged her breasts like a worn-out lover. He couldn't stop his breath from whistling a bit faster as the sleep shirt peaked over her nipples before dropping to caress the slight swell of her stomach, then continued at breakneck speed to the apex of her thighs, before finally ending enticingly several inches above her knees. By the time J.D.'s eyes had completely finished the journey, he could feel the buttons of his jeans starting to strain against his rising flesh. Since satisfying his sudden desire was impossible, he took refuge in humor. "I can't say I'm too disappointed by your choice of duds, honey. Just surprised."

"Honey!" Rebecca squeaked as her eyes got even bigger.

"Sorry…Rebecca, I mean." J.D. grinned as she rapidly crossed her arms over her chest. His comment had obviously reminded her that she was standing in front of a virtual stranger in the middle of the night in a T-shirt, regardless of what it looked like. Unable to resist the urge to touch her, J.D. rubbed the inside of her arm, choosing the sensitive area in the crook of her elbow. He was pleased to see goose bumps raise immediately. "Are you cold?"

"No, I'm not cold!" She scowled even as she shivered. "You scared me to death!"

"Hush, now." Not paying any attention to her as she tried to push him away, he placed his palms on her arms and briskly rubbed them up and down to bring some of the color back to her face—color now going from white to a flushed rosy pink. "Just relax." Automatically his voice dropped another octave, taking on the tone he used to settle high-strung horses.

"I can't relax when you're touching me."

Surprised at her admission, his eyes opened wide. His gaze flew to hers but she had lowered her lids. J.D. studied the black lashes, so long they cast shadows onto her cheeks. He lifted his hands and stepped backward. "I must admit, it's not too relaxing for me, either."

At that her lashes flew upward and brilliant blue eyes pierced his. For a moment they were both silent as they exchanged a rueful glance. Obviously this day had been a bit more than both of them had expected. J.D. wasn't sure what her expectations had been when she'd showed up at his door, but he certainly hadn't expected to have two females force themselves into his all male domain today. He thrust a hand through his hair and changed the subject. "What was wrong with the baby?"

Rebecca gasped. "The baby." She sent a harried look toward her bedroom. "Her teeth, I think. I was going to look in your medicine cabinet to see—"

"I did pick up something recently for the toothache I had a last month. A paregoric. That stuff numbs everything it touches. Think that would work on a baby?"

"I don't see why not. At least it's worth a try."

His mind now occupied with other matters, he absently patted Rebecca's shoulder. "Run on back to the room and I'll see if I can track it down in the bathroom. I'll be there in a minute."

Rebecca nodded and returned to her room. When J.D. pulled up in the doorway a moment later, she was looking down at Jessie, who was a visible outline as the light from the hallway spilled over the bed. To J.D.'s surprise, the baby seemed to be sleeping.

"Why don't you try it on your lip or something first?"

"On my lip?" The woman must have lost her mind while he was gone.

Rebecca folded her arms like a teacher confronting a stubborn student. "Well, J.D., what if it's been spoiled or something? We have to test it before we try it on a baby."

"Why don't we test it on your lip? You're probably a better judge of what's right for babies." No way did J.D. want numb lips for the rest of the night.

Rebecca narrowed her eyes, then obviously decided it wasn't worth the trouble to argue so she turned to face him and puckered up. Faced with such a tempting prospect, J.D.'s mind immediately wandered into more pleasant realms, but a brisk throat clearing by Rebecca recalled his attention. "Right. Here goes, then." He upended the bottle onto his fingertip and stroked it over her full bottom lip. "How's that?"

"Mmm…hmmm…"

He leaned closer, peering at her mouth as if he were expecting to see smoke or something. "Feel anything yet?"

The tip of Rebecca's tongue hesitantly stroked her lower lip. "It's kinda… I can't tell if…"

Without warning, J.D. swooped to press a quick kiss on her lips. Why he did it, he wasn't sure. Except she looked so damn appealing standing there in her college sleep shirt, with her eyes all wide and hesitant and her sleek hairdo flying every which way. She reminded him of a young filly, ripe for maturity but lacking the knowledge of life. Funny she should strike him that way—her being a big-time career woman and him more used to having hard earth than hard cement under his boots—but it was what he felt when he looked at her. Maybe it was the slight uncertainty he saw in her eyes, or the way her shoulders tensed right before she slapped him down with a sassy comeback. Whatever it was, she brought out instincts that confused him.

He lifted his lips from hers and immediately stepped backward before she could take a swing at him. But he need not have worried. She was too thunderstruck to move. J.D. decided to lighten the moment. "Did you feel that?"

"Yes…no…I don't know." Her eyebrows snapped together and her nose scrunched up in such adorable confusion that J.D. was tempted to kiss her again. However a mutter from Jessie distracted him.

"Uh-oh. She's moving again." He lifted Rebecca's hand and slapped the bottle into her palm. "Why don't you rub some of this stuff on her gums? Then she'll probably go right back to sleep."

Rebecca immediately knelt by the baby and soothed her as she rubbed a gentle finger over Jessie's gums. Then she adjusted the pillows around the little body and covered her with a light sheet. She stepped back to J.D.'s side. Silently they watched the baby stop squirming and take a deep sigh to relax back into sleep. Reaching over Rebecca's shoulders, J.D. took the bottle and recapped it. He slipped it into his pocket. "Mission accomplished."

"Yes." Rebecca sent him a tiny smile, which faded as she grabbed her mid-section. "…ooohhh!"

"What is it?"

A delicate pink stained her cheeks and she doubled over to clench her stomach. "I…I have a stomach ache."

He pulled her out of the room and into the hallway. Slinging an arm around her shoulder, he took her weight against him for a moment. "What do you think? Is it the flu or something?"

Rebecca sent him a killing glance from under her lashes. "My money's on the stew, not the flu."

That surprised a short laugh from J.D. He instantly apologized as she glared at him. He moved them farther away from the open door so they didn't disturb the baby. "Sorry. I hadn't considered the stew. I've been eating it for years and it's never bothered me."

"Well, obviously you're used to it. I'm used to skinless baked chicken and steamed vegetables." She doubled over again, clutching her stomach.

Grimacing at her comment, he patted her shoulder. "No wonder you're so peaked. You need more good Texas beef in that diet of yours.'' He took her hand and tried to pull her toward the steps. "Come on."

Insulted, Rebecca lifted her head to comment, "There is nothing wrong with a healthy diet—"

"We'll talk about it later. Come with me." She resisted moving and started to give him a mini-lecture on the virtues of lean meat, so J.D. didn't bother to disagree with her. He settled the issue by scooping her into his arms, the same way he used to do with his sister when she was being difficult. "We're going to fix you right up." He headed for the stairs.

"Stop. I can't leave the baby. I haven't set up the baby monitor yet."

"The door's open. We'll hear her if she wakes up."

"J. D. McCoy, put me down this minute."

"Don't kick, you'll knock me off balance."

To J.D.'s relief, Rebecca stopped kicking when she looked down and saw the long line of stairs extending below her. Startling him, she threw her arms tightly around his neck. He coughed. "Don't strangle me, either. I'm not going to drop you."

"I'm not comfortable being carried around like a sack of animal feed." She gritted her teeth as another spasm swept over her. Finally she gasped, "Where are we going?"

He smiled down at her. "To make a relaxing cup of chamomile-and-peppermint tea. That's what my mama always gave me when I had a bad stomach ache."

He reached the bottom of the stairs and strode through the hall to the kitchen. He deposited her on the counter, where she sat uncomfortably with her legs dangling. Another spasm had her doubling over again as he checked the kettle. "Hold on Reb, you'll be right and tight soon." J.D. grabbed a long match and lit the burner before returning to the counter to rummage around. He unearthed a small glass jar of dried herbs from the many on the counter next to the sink.

Rebecca straightened and took a deep breath. "It's not labeled. How do you know what it is?"

"I'm used to them. My mama believed in using herbs for everything—doctoring, cooking." He gave the lid a quick twist. "For some reason Smoke feels bound to carry on Ma's tradition. He's always adding a pinch of this 'n a pinch of that to whatever he's cooking. Never writes it down, though, so nothing ever tastes the same way twice."

Rebecca's hand on his arm got his attention. He stopped measuring a small amount of herbs into a tea strainer to look at her questioningly. "You mean I'm never going to know what I'm eating?" she asked.

His hand patted hers. "Don't you fret, Reb. I'm not going to have you wandering the hall every night. It's too hard on me." At least it would be if she didn't get some long flannel pajamas. His blood pressure was still pounding in his ears as Rebecca sat there, rubbing her stomach and trying to pretend that sitting on an old wooden counter in the middle of the night in her nightgown was commonplace. When she tried ineffectively to control a shiver, he put the mugs he'd just gotten from the cupboard down and walked to the kitchen door.

"Where are you going?" She wiggled off the counter and stepped toward him.

The note of panic surprised him...and touched him. He didn't much like that. He thought they'd get along better if she was tart and tangy instead of vulnerable. J.D. didn't want her to be vulnerable. He didn't do too well with vulnerable. Vulnerable required the ability to completely open up and respond to someone else's need. He'd been keeping his heart locked up for a long time now, and no woman, no matter how attractive, was going to change that.

"Don't worry. I'm going into the mudroom for a minute," he soothed. "I'll be right back."

Opening the door, J.D. stepped inside to find something to cover her up. He located one of his just-washed denim shirts over by the washer. Slinging it over his shoulder he stepped back into the kitchen. He walked over to her, first checking the stove where the kettle was bubbling merrily.

"Here you go." J.D. held the shirt for her as she turned to slip her arms into the sleeves. "It gets cooler after sundown, and that cotton thing you're wearing doesn't look too warm."

Flushing, Rebecca said, "You must think I'm an idiot."

"Course not." J.D. understood having fears that wouldn't seem too rational in the daylight. God knew he had them.

"I didn't mean to panic before." She sent an uneasy glance toward the windows by the table. "It's so dark here at night. I'm used to city lights. Cities are never really dark, you know."

"I know." He'd been in enough cities to know every time he went, he couldn't wait to shake the grime from his heels and come back to the land that nurtured his soul. He could appreciate other people's love for the bright lights and excitement, but after a while, he longed for home. He wondered if she'd ever experienced that longing. He took their mugs over to the stove and poured the hot water into the cups. "Being out here takes a bit of getting used to. But on the other hand, the stars are the brightest you've ever seen. You never really see them in the city."

"I don't pay much attention to the stars in Boston."

"Is that where you're from? Boston? You don't have much of an accent."

"That's because I wasn't born there." She took the tea he handed her and followed him over to the table, careful to take a seat that didn't place her back to the dark expanse outside the glass. "Thanks for—"

J.D. lifted his mug and saluted her. "No thanks necessary. Just good old Texas hospitality. My daddy would have walloped my bottom if I didn't help out somebody in need.''

"That must have been nice.''

"No ma'am, it wasn't.'' J.D. laughed, softly. "My daddy was a big man and when he took a strap to me, I generally deserved it.'' He'd never resented it either, because he knew his dad didn't take the action lightly.

Rebecca sipped her tea and smiled. "I meant the hospitality and helping part was nice.''

"That's the way it is when your nearest neighbor is about twenty miles away.'' He took a big gulp of tea and urged her to drink hers. "How's your stomach feeling?''

"A bit better. I don't know if it's your mother's remedy, or whether it was calming down anyway, but I'm glad.''

"Don't worry, I won't tell Smoke his cooking kept you up all night.''

Rebecca looked around the kitchen. "Where does Smoke sleep? In the bunkhouse? Didn't one of you mention a bunkhouse?''

"Smoke's got nice, cozy quarters off the mudroom over there. It used to be the summer kitchen 'til I remodeled it for him.'' J.D. jerked a thumb toward the door. "He moved out of the bunkhouse when he stopped the hard ranch work.''

Wrinkling her nose, Rebecca asked, "Why'd he stop? That doesn't seem in character from what I've seen.''

"I stopped him. His arthritis was getting worse. He wouldn't admit it, but riding the range, mending fences and working with the stock was getting mighty hard on him. Last year I moved him indoors. You would have thought I'd gelded him.'' J.D. laughed, then sobered. "Although in a way I guess I did, when I gave him a stove to ride instead of a horse. But…that old man means a lot to me. I couldn't see him suffering and too proud to admit it. So, I took the decision out of his hands.''

Rebecca smiled. "How'd he feel about that?''

J.D. rolled his eyes. "How do you think? He's spent all his life working here with my family and he felt as if I'd put him out to pasture. I had to do some fancy talking to get him to agree." He looked at her over the brim of his mug. "Then you showed up. You and a baby."

"I'll take care of myself and Jessie. We won't be much bother."

"Oh, no," he drawled, giving her a sardonic look, thinking of the baby's activity and hers since they'd arrived. "I'm sure you won't be any bother at all. Little crying babies and good-looking women never cause any trouble." He pulled his gaze from hers and stared into the darkness beyond the window for a long moment. "I've gotta tell you...your timing's not too good, Rebecca. I've got about all the responsibility I can handle at the moment. I've been busting my butt for years to make this ranch profitable again and I'm just starting to turn the corner."

"I understand."

J.D. pulled his gaze from the night pressing against the window. "Do you? Do you know what it's like to scrimp and save and work your fingers to the bone, for something you might lose anyway?" He studied her, from her chic hairstyle and manicure, to the indefinably classy way she wore her old college allegiance. "No offense...Rebecca... but you look a bit too expensive to understand that."

With a self-conscious gesture, she touched her stylish haircut. "I can't help that. That's what I was brought up with—" she bit her lip "—well, most of my life, anyway. Then halfway through college I discovered I wanted to give back to people...instead of just taking. That's why I went into social work."

"Social work?" Leaning his elbow on the table, he turned to face her full on. "Okay, now that there's no little baby around to distract us, let's talk about Rosalie. What happened to her?"

Rebecca placed her mug on the table and laced her fingers together. Glancing toward the window, she admitted, "I really don't know."

"Why don't you know? Weren't you assigned to her?"

She met his gaze then. "Not assigned exactly. I've been working with her for the past four months."

"Working with her how?"

Rebecca picked at a fingernail. "I guess I was burning out in my job, so a little while ago my boss transferred me into a new role. I'm helping new mothers learn how to care for their babies…learn to handle difficulties and take positive action, that sort of thing."

J.D. narrowed his eyes at the woman across the table. So, she was pretty new at the job herself. That explained a lot. It certainly explained why she seemed rather awkward handling the baby herself. "Let me get this straight. You were helping Rosalie learn responsibility?"

"I guess you could call it that. I was teaching her about motherhood and family…"

"And you know all about that, huh?" He wondered if there was a child lurking in her background, or even a husband. He checked her hand to be certain he hadn't missed a ring.

Her face heated as she looked away from him. "Not… exactly. I'm not a nurse, and I don't have any personal experience, but I've had additional training and I've read a lot."

He leaned back in his chair and stretched an arm along the table, studying her like a bug under a microscope. "So, you were teaching Rosalie all about taking care of her baby when she up and left her on your doorstep." He was trying to keep the blame from his voice. After all, he knew better than anyone how impossible Rosalie could be when she got a burr under her saddle. But it was difficult not to be angry. He hated the thought of Rosalie out there alone…. He tried to push the images from his mind. Finally he drawled, "If

Rosalie is your first client, you're not too successful at your new job are you?''

Her skin paled. She folded her arms, hugging them around her waist. "No," she whispered, "that's why I'm here. To fix that.''

"Sorry." J.D. made an apologetic gesture as he saw her distress. "That was uncalled for.''

"That's okay. I deserve it.''

Studying her hunched shoulders, he said, "Knowing my sister, that's debatable.''

J.D. thought of Rosalie as he had last seen her. Then he thought of the baby he'd just seen this evening. He'd loved his sister, but he wasn't sure he could forgive her. When she left she'd taken every ounce of faith he'd had. He didn't feel he had any love to give anymore, not after he'd freely given it away only to have it thrown back in his face a few times. Even so, he was worried sick about Rosalie, though he wouldn't admit it. *What kind of trouble had made her leave a helpless baby?* Finally J.D. leaned forward, rubbing his forehead with a tired hand. "Rebecca, some things can't be fixed." Wishing it were different didn't make it any better...or easier. Not when the ties had been ripped apart and thrown to the wind.

"I can't accept that, J.D. I truly believe Rosalie will be back for this child. I think she'll come back because she has something to settle with you as well as herself.''

He thrust his chin forward, saying forcefully, "After running out on me and the ranch, the only thing she has left to settle is where she's going to live with this kid." If Rosalie did come back he wasn't going to make it easy on her. He tore his gaze from Rebecca's. He could tell by her compassionate expression that his hurt and frustration were fully apparent. He hated that. He preferred to keep dirty family laundry private, not hang it out for the world to see. He'd let this woman see too much already. "Where the hell's the father, anyway?''

"I don't know. Rosalie didn't say." Rebecca lifted her shoulders. "I don't even know who he is."

"Well, Jessie oughta be with him, not me. That's what should happen."

"J.D., be reasonable, sometimes relationships don't work out." Spreading her arms wide, Rebecca gently continued, "Trust me, I'm an expert on that. But Rosalie is your family. That's why I came."

He rose to his feet. "Did it ever occur to you that I might have been married? Or getting married so there wouldn't be room for her here?"

Rebecca stood to face him. "You're getting married?"

"God, no." That was one disaster he'd managed to avoid at least.

Her face mirrored her relief. "Then there's no problem."

It was clear to J.D. that she hadn't even considered that possibility. "Yes, there is. You're going to stay here for a few weeks, but then what?" He grabbed his mug and strode across the linoleum to place it in the sink. "What if, despite what you think, Rosalie has cut and run for good? Did you ever think of that?"

"No…not exactly."

"Well, you should have." He spun around and started to pace, his long strides devouring the kitchen linoleum. "God, I don't understand this. I did all I could for my sister."

"Maybe she needed more."

J.D. glanced over his shoulder. A harsh laugh forced itself from his throat. "Who didn't? After our mom died, my life was all about Rosalie and the ranch. There was little time for anything else." He shoved his hands through his hair, and continued to cover the kitchen from one end to another. "Hell, my own girl blew me off because of it." He stopped, appalled that the words had burst out of him despite his intention to keep quiet. He tried to recover by facing her and taking a challenging stance, fists knuckled on his waist, hips thrust forward. "So you see—and I don't mean to give offense—but at this moment, I don't need any more women in my life. Not a sister, a social worker…or a baby."

Rebecca licked her lips. "I'm sorry, J.D. If I'd known the way things really are, I wouldn't have come." She rose and carried her mug to the sink. "I thought…well it doesn't matter what I thought. We'll just have to deal with the problem, if it arises, as best we can."

"How do you suggest we do that?"

Rebecca was silent for a long moment. Then she looked up and gave him a confident smile, that wavered a bit as she met his gaze. "Don't worry. I'll come up with something. I'm very resourceful. In the meantime, I promise you'll scarcely know we're around."

4

Rebecca woke up the next morning determined to break her word. She'd promised she and Jessie wouldn't trouble Uncle J.D. at all. Wrong! Rebecca was determined to mold these two into the start of a family unit if it killed her. Someone had to do it. She might not have had much experience with a functional family herself, but she knew what it should contain—love, trust and sharing. She was positive J.D. had all those qualities. It was just up to her to somehow bring them out.

Refusing to acknowledge that her plan to immerse J.D. in his niece's life seemed rosy in the extreme, if not downright naive, Rebecca rolled over in the bed. Stretching her arms over her head, she extended her legs and stared at one of J.D.'s high school football trophies. She wasn't surprised to see proof that he'd been a good athlete when he was younger. He had the look of a winner, and not just physically. He had the concentration and toughness needed to excel. Then she thought of J. D. McCoy as she'd seen him last night, and realized she'd seen a different man than his high school promise had suggested. She'd seen a man tempered by circumstances...at once tender and competent, then frustrated and aggressive. All in all, J. D. McCoy was a formidable package. She wouldn't want to be on his bad side. Come to think of it, she didn't envy Rosalie McCoy when she got back, either. There was a lot of hurt there.

Hurt that could easily erupt into a white-hot anger. Not violence—Rebecca didn't get that impression. But the kind of anger that ripped jagged tears into relationships forever if it wasn't channeled correctly. God knew, she'd seen enough of it over the years. Enough so, it made her wonder if any family could ever really make it. At this point, she'd seen too much and felt the pain of failure too many times to think seriously about making that commitment herself.

Could Rosalie have deceived me? After all, she had lied about her relationship with her brother. Rebecca bit her fingernail before a lifetime of her mother yelling about ladies having lovely nails reasserted itself. She hated to admit it, but she should develop a contingency plan. Maybe find the nearest town and newspaper and check the classifieds for child care specialists.

That decided, she sat up and looked down at Jessie, who was starting to murmur. *No crying or fussing, thank goodness.* Rebecca smiled. In the few days she'd been with her, Rebecca discovered she loved listening to early-morning baby sounds. The day was all fresh and new and babies sensed that. There was a whole new adventure to be lived. That thought excited Rebecca as well. A whole new adventure for her, too? It felt like it. She had that goose-bumpy feeling—like something was going to jump out and grab her.

A sharp whistle startled her and she scrambled to her knees to look out the window above the bed. Her breath caught in her throat as she peered through the glass. There was something so right about the sight of a black-and-white dog racing across the open fields toward a lone horseman, that she smiled in appreciation. Was that J.D.? Rebecca watched the man and horse move as one with an elemental power and raw beauty that matched the landscape.

And some would call this land beautiful. Rosalie had when she'd talked about home. There had been a longing in her voice that Rebecca had envied.

However, Rosalie had not mentioned the pain she'd obviously caused her brother. Regardless of his lighthearted humor, the man tried to keep things well hidden. Rebecca had a feeling he was like the land he lived on—she would have to dig deep to find the true sweetness. She was surprised at how appealing she found that.

After all, she knew nothing about J.D., not really. He was the other side of the coin as far as she was concerned. He was a man suited to the sparsely populated spaces, while she generally had an allergic reaction if she was too far away from crowded sidewalks for any length of time. Not that she didn't appreciate nature. She did. But beyond the cement that surrounded her parents town house—or penthouse, at the moment—and the lake she used to visit as a child, her acquaintance with the soil was limited to well-manicured lawns. She cast a last look at the vanishing rider as he rode across the limitless landscape toward the place where the sky kissed the earth. Beautiful it might be, but the vast size of Texas scared her.

Rebecca turned from the window, checked Jessie, who'd fallen back to sleep, and raced to the bathroom for a fast washup. Coming back to the room, she rummaged through her suitcase for something cool. If yesterday was anything to go by it would get very hot today. Of course it would! she thought with a wry grimace. She was in Texas in the middle of summer! What did she expect?

Rebecca pulled out a pair of stone-colored shorts and a short-sleeve yellow pullover. Dressing quickly, she was stepping into a pair of brown sandals when a noise behind her made her look around. She peeked over her shoulder. Jessie was awake. Her little fingers were laced together as she twisted her body and craned her neck to watch every movement Rebecca made. Jessie's eyes were as wide as the just risen sun and as bright as the morning sky.

"Hi, Jessie."

Charmed, Rebecca smiled as the baby wriggled in response to her name. Even though Rebecca helped inexperienced mothers learn how to handle their motherhood, her hours were generally nine to five. This was only the second time she'd ever awakened to find one in the same room with her. Even if the night before had left something to be desired, it was a delightful experience.

Rebecca walked over to the trundle bed and sat down. Placing one finger on Jessie's nose she said, "Hello, you little monkey." Rebecca laughed as the baby squirmed with delight and screwed up her face to make a noise in response. After a few minutes of playing, Rebecca pulled the baby's bag over to the bed. As she changed Jessie, she said, "I think you should look as cute as possible when you see your uncle again today. He's not too happy to have us here."

Rebecca glanced down at her own outfit, thinking it probably wouldn't be a bad idea for her, either. With a disgusted snort, she dismissed the thought. What she looked like didn't matter, only Jessie did. Besides, the man had practically seen her in her underwear the night before and managed to keep himself under control. So, there was no reason to think he'd be any more susceptible to female wiles in the daylight. Not that she'd stoop to using anything as obvious as that to make him accept their presence here. She probably wouldn't be very good at it, anyway.

Placing Jessie into the infant seat, she strapped her in, leaving her kicking happily. Then Rebecca straightened the beds. As she smoothed the sheets and quilt, she couldn't help imagining J.D. lying there, dreaming the dreams of all young men. Not that Rebecca knew what form those dreams would have taken. She was an only child and had no experience of brothers or male cousins or anything that shed tons of light onto the male psyche. However, her psychology training gave her theories galore. Enough so, she felt she understood men's needs and desires...in an abstract fashion. She dealt with some of the results of those desires every day at work.

"Okay, pumpkin, time for breakfast." Rebecca slung the diaper bag over her shoulder, picked up the baby seat and left the room. She made her way down the hall, casting a quick peek toward the hallway where she'd been surprised by J.D. She'd been touched by his actions last night. That worried her a bit. Much as she was tempted—after all he was a beautiful male—she didn't want to see him as anything more than Jessie's uncle. "I need to keep this situation strictly professional." A sharp sound emerged from her lips as she realized the absurdity she'd muttered.

Nothing about this situation was professional.

Last night she'd been sitting in a kitchen wearing her nightshirt, with a half-naked man sitting opposite her. How professional was that? Not to mention that she was here without any authority whatsoever.

Holding the infant seat close against her body, Rebecca picked her way down the steps. The vestibule didn't look any neater in the morning than it had in the evening. To her surprise, her fingers itched for a dust cloth and polish. The rich wood of the banister and wainscoting would be lovely if it were cleaned. "Looks like we'll have lots to do later today, Jessie."

Then the heavenly aroma of coffee distracted her. For a moment she inhaled and felt her eyelids move one step closer to full mast. Rebecca hurried toward the kitchen and swung through the door. She pulled up short at the sight of Smoke in his familiar position by the side of the stove. He was hunched over another pot, stirring madly.

"Morning." Rebecca directed a disapproving frown at Smoke's dangling cigarette.

To her surprise he cast her a stricken look, then plucked the butt from his lips and dropped it onto the brick floor surrounding the stove. "Sorry, I forgot." He crushed it under his heel. "Dang habit."

Rebecca decided to ignore that bit of untidiness, saying warmly, "Thank you, Smoke." Along with the coffee, another scent rose into the air when Smoke lifted the lid off the saucepan and placed it aside. Rebecca sniffed and pointed at a large saucepan. "What's that?"

"Breakfast."

She stepped closer to run a wary eye over the steaming mess in the pot. She gulped, remembering how Smoke's stew of unknown origin had affected her last night. Then she told herself to knock it off. After all, last night's stew also looked rather awful, but had been tasty. Unfortunately she didn't have as much hope for this concoction. "Uh, what's in it?"

Smoke pursed his lips, finally saying, "Some of this and some of that."

His answer alarmed her. She could just imagine what some of this and some of that would do to her digestion. Her customary tact deserted her. "Good thing I'm not hungry." Of course, just at the moment her stomach let out a growl worthy of a Bengal tiger in snowstorm.

After an amused look, Smoke shrugged. "Suit yourself, but it's my special recipe." He hitched himself across the linoleum to get his coffee mug and went back to the stove to refill it. Picking up his spoon, Smoke jammed it into the kettle again.

Jessie started to murmur, so Rebecca absently rocked the baby to quiet her. She glanced down at Jessie, now loudly sucking her fingers. Rebecca ignored her own stomach and said instead, "The baby's hungry, though."

Smoke lifted his spoon. A lump of what looked like drippy playdough resided in the middle of it. "This here gruel is just the thing for a young'un."

Incredulously Rebecca stared at the spoon. She had a funny feeling that aesthetic cooking and Smoke had no acquaintance. Hadn't anyone told him that presentation was half of the meal? "Thanks, but no gruel for this young one…or this old one, either. I'll make Jessie baby cereal and fix a bottle.''

For a moment they stared at each other, each staking out their position. Finally Rebecca sent him an appealing smile. It wouldn't help to get him annoyed with her, any more than he probably already was. Obviously J.D.'s was not the only life she'd interrupted when she and Jessie barreled onto the ranch. She hadn't thought about that before she'd impulsively set off for Texas. She needed an ally, so she smiled again. "I'd definitely like some of that delicious smelling coffee."

Smoke reached above the stove and pulled a mug from a shelf. He lifted the battered campsite metal pot and poured her a cup.

Rebecca almost swooned at the sight of the hot, brown liquid. Walking over to the counter, she placed the infant seat well back from the edge while taking the coffee from Smoke. She inhaled. The aroma started parts of her brain she'd forgotten existed until this moment. Rebecca took a tiny sip, not quite trusting Smoke's coffee making skill anymore than his other ones. But she did him an injustice. "Ooh, this is delicious."

Smoke sent her an incredulous look. "Course it is. If there's anything a Texan knows how to do, it's make a cup of coffee that'll wake you up from the dead."

"Great. I didn't sleep too well."

"The pot's always on, missy. So you help yourself to that whenever you want."

A whimper from Jessie attracted her attention. "All right, sweetie. Breakfast time." She put her cup down, then unslung the diaper bag from her shoulder and started to prepare Jessie's meal.

"Waste of money, if you ask me, spending good cash on those little boxes of food. Time was, good home cooking is all a babe needed…that and a big splash of mama's milk.''

That surprised a chuckle from Rebecca. "Well, I do need some milk to mix in this cereal but..." She glanced down at her chest then mischievously up at Smoke. "I'm afraid I'm going to have to get it from a bottle. Then heat it up."

Smoke almost grinned at her then covered it by carefully folding his lips into a straight line. He pointed at the fridge. "Milk's in the icebox over there." Walking over to hand her a saucepan, he stepped carefully up to the infant seat.

"She won't bite," Rebecca said.

"That's not what I saw last night."

He stared at the baby. "She's got a look of that pesky Rosalie, right around the eyes and the mouth."

"Keep an eye on her for a minute, okay?" Rebecca scooted over to the fridge and dumped some milk into the pan. With a glance over her shoulder to check on Jessie, who was babbling to Smoke, she walked to the stove. Perplexed, she studied the big black monstrosity. "I have an electric stove at home. Where's the burner?"

Smoke snorted. "Dang waste of money those electric things. If I can't have a campfire, I'll take this old wood stove any day. Just put it on the stovetop."

"This is a wood stove?" Rebecca recoiled, feeling as if she'd just confronted a dinosaur in the parlor. Gingerly, she placed the pan on the flat top of the cookstove, right in front of the pot of nastiness Smoke was cooking.

At that moment, J.D. blasted his way into the room from the enclosed porch, swearing a blue streak followed by, "I need some coffee, Smoke. That damn herd of cattle busted through the fence again in the north pasture." He skidded to a stop and blinked. His glance raced from Rebecca to the baby who had started to yell at his noisy intrusion, then back again to Rebecca.

"Well...this is...different." He was obviously trying to process the reality of two females in his kitchen first thing in the morning. He pushed his hat back. "Like someone else's house."

He suddenly looked so confused that Rebecca had to swallow a grin. He was no longer the self-possessed man she'd run into in the middle of the night. After all, he'd probably expected to sit down peacefully with a cup of coffee, not walk into bedlam. If she'd wanted to disrupt his life she couldn't have planned it better. Although she didn't intend for it to be this noisy!

J.D. cast an appalled eye in Jessie's direction and yelled, "She still getting a tooth?"

Rebecca moved to quiet Jessie. "She's going to get a lot of them, but I don't think that's the problem at the moment."

"You take care of the young'un, missy," Smoke almost ran her down trying to put distance between himself and the crying baby, "and I'll take care of the milk."

J.D. closed his eyes for a minute, then said loudly, "What's the matter with her, then?"

Rebecca tried patting Jessie, to no avail. "Babies aren't crazy about loud noises. You scared her when you came in like a herd of buffalo." She thrust her arm out. "Smoke, hurry."

Smoke promptly slapped the bottle into her hand. She tested it for temperature and shoved it into Jessie's mouth. After another token yell the baby latched onto the nipple and sucked. For a moment the noisy gulp was the only thing heard in the kitchen.

"By God, I've got to remember that trick," J.D. breathed.

Rebecca smiled at him over her shoulder. "Me, too." With one hand she held the bottle in place, dumping the cereal in a bowl with the other.

"J.D., could you give me some help for a moment?"

J.D. backed up with a wary look. "I, uh…have to…"

Rebecca indicated the baby. "Just hold this bottle while I finish making her food."

"Just hold it? Not feed her anything?" He stared at the

baby, seeming to consider that for a moment before stepping backward. "You know, I really have to get back to the cattle."

Rebecca realized that in the light of day he seemed very reluctant to get involved. She'd taken him by surprise last night, but he'd obviously spent some of the morning erecting his own fences. She wasn't sure if they were against the baby—or her.

Rebecca smiled her kindest smile. "Never mind, J.D. I don't want to interfere with your ranch work." Not much she didn't! "Run along. I can manage here."

J.D. backed toward the door. "Well, good. I'll see you later…maybe." With that, he turned on his heel and bolted from the kitchen.

Rebecca turned to Smoke. "Did I say something wrong?"

Smoke removed his hat, scratched his head, and immediately jammed the hat back on his head. "Danged if I know. I ain't seen that boy move so fast since a randy bull charged a cow and he was in the line of fire."

"I realize we're in the way here, but—"

"Don't fret now, missy. You're right. This young'un belongs here." Smoke came over and took the bottle from Rebecca's hand. "J.D. knows it. He just needs some time to get used to the idea."

Rebecca studied the grizzled old cowboy next to her. Why hadn't she noticed the laugh lines around his eyes before? "Do you think he'll get used to it?"

Smoke grinned, a big, wide toothless grin. "Not without some help. Why don't you take him some coffee? I can get food into this child's mouth."

Rebecca stopped mixing Jessie's cereal. She sent him a suspicious look. "You're not going to give her your special breakfast stuff are you?"

Smoke laughed. "Well, seeing as how that's slop I was cooking up for the pigs—"

"Why you…" Rebecca's jaw dropped until she could almost trip over it. Then she started to laugh.

"I never could resist playing a joke on a city slicker." Smoke indicated the door. "Now, you get outta here. Go take a look at Texas in the morning…'n don't let J.D. run you off the place, Missy. 'Cause he's gonna try. You sneak up on him, then stand your ground."

J.D. didn't slow down until he'd put as much distance as he possibly could between himself and the ranch house. His boot heels kicked up dry, dusty puffs of dirt as he jerked to a stop outside the barn door. Looking at the knotted, weathered wood, he wondered how he'd gotten there. One minute he'd been contemplating a nice, tongue-burning cup of coffee and the next—

He slammed the heel of his palm against his forehead. *What the hell was the matter with him?* He couldn't believe a woman and a pint-size infant had sent him into full retreat without even firing a shot. He wasn't that disturbed about seeing them here, was he? Obviously he was. His lips twisted as he made fun of himself for hightailing it out of the house like an outraged, gun-toting father was right behind him.

J.D. tried to justify his cowardly actions to himself. After all, he hadn't expected to see them this morning. He'd thought Rebecca Chandler, not being used to ranch life, would still be asleep. He'd figured the baby, being up with teething problems during the night, would sleep late, too…which showed how much he knew about infants. As if he needed more proof of his ignorance. But no, there they were—big as life in his kitchen, and he'd panicked.

A cold nose shoved itself into his palm and he jumped. "Damn, Biscuit. Don't sneak up on me like that." He scowled down at his dog, who cocked her head to give him an inquiring stare. J.D. responded to the friendly look by sighing and scratching Biscuit's ears, one of which comically stood straight up while the other drooped as if it needed a transfusion. A slight noise attracted his attention and he glimpsed a flash of movement from the corner of his eye.

"What type of dog is that?"

J.D. and Biscuit turned as one to regard the woman standing behind them. "A Border collie."

"Pretty. I like the black-and-white markings." Rebecca handed him a pottery mug. "Here. I thought you might need this."

Automatically he took it. "Thanks. I do." He inhaled the deep, rich aroma which competed pleasantly with the scents of the barnyard around him.

Indicating the dog's drooping ear, Rebecca asked, "Is its ear supposed to do that?"

"That's what gives my dog personality."

Rebecca hesitated, then held her hand out to the dog. "He, uh...won't bite or anything, will he?"

"Not unless you're a cow." J.D. took a laconic sip of his coffee. "And then *she* only nips."

Rebecca started to withdraw her hand, then, with a narrow look at him, extended it again to the dog. Biscuit glanced at her master for permission before stepping forward. Rebecca seemed to force herself to stand still, but her nose wrinkled as the animal started to lick her fingers then rapidly proceeded to drench the rest of her hand. When the dog had finished she kept her fingers extended as if she didn't know what to do with them. "Oh my, she's... friendly, isn't she?"

"Biscuit isn't too neat, but she's enthusiastic." J.D. chuckled before reaching his arm toward her. "Here, wipe your hand on my sleeve."

With a strange look at him, she did so. "I've never had a dog."

"No, really?" J.D. couldn't help teasing her, even as his

arm still tingled from the feeling of her fingers stroking his shirt.

She smiled as she kept a rather nervous eye on the dog at her feet. "My mother never let me have any pets. She said they were too much trouble."

"Well, they are. They're a lot of trouble, but they're worth it. At least, I think they are." He couldn't imagine anyone having a life without animals.

He studied Rebecca as he lifted his mug to his lips. Taking a slow sip, he gave her the once-over. In her hot-weather clothing, she looked a lot different from the crisp woman who'd arrived at his ranch last evening—but she still didn't look like she belonged. No, casually dressed or not, she had *sophistication* written all over her in capital letters. He let his gaze travel from her tasteful scoop-neck top, down her trim shorts to her brown sandals that revealed shockingly painted toenails. He took another sip of coffee. Blazing red toenails didn't seem to fit the rest of the image. J.D. found that fascinating. As he stared, she scrunched her toes, trying to make them less obvious.

"Biscuit is an interesting name for a dog. Why did you name her Biscuit?"

Amused by her diversionary tactics, J.D. lifted his gaze from her toenails. "Well, now…when she was a puppy she invented all kinds of ways to sneak one of Smoke's pan biscuits. Smoke kept yelling, 'Get away from them biscuits, dog.' But she didn't." J.D. shrugged and finished the last of his coffee before adding, "Finally the name Biscuit stuck." Biscuit wagged her tail in the dirt as she stared first at one then the other. "Didn't it, girl?" Biscuit's ear's became even more lopsided as she grinned a wide dog smile, then punctuated the conversation with one happy *woof.*

Rebecca smiled. "She looks too smart to want to eat Smoke's cooking." Then to J.D.'s surprise she flushed, saying rapidly, "I'm sorry, that was really rude. I didn't mean to—"

Laughing, J.D. flung some leftover coffee grounds into the dirt, then set the mug down on a nearby bench. "No need to apologize. Some of Smoke's dishes have to grow on you."

"I know. I've had that experience."

She sent him a look that made him remember last night all the way to his toes. He wasn't sure they were remembering the same thing, though. His thoughts still shimmered with visions of her long legs, soft curves and the way her long, dark lashes had cast shadows on her cheeks.

To escape his thoughts and his body's uncomfortable response, J.D. walked over to the corral railing. He hooked the heel of his boot on the rung behind him and leaned back against the fence. Biscuit seemed torn between following him and staying near her new friend. Finally, after bumping Rebecca's hand with her nose as if to reassure her she wanted to be her friend, Biscuit compromised by creeping over to the doorway of the barn and collapsing with a sigh.

"Biscuit seems to like you."

Rebecca stared at the collie, then pulled her gaze back to J.D. "I haven't the vaguest idea why. I don't know a thing about dogs."

"Dogs are a good judge of character. And working dogs, like Biscuit, are smart as hell! I'd rather lose my best girl than lose Biscuit."

"I thought you didn't want a girlfriend."

He yanked his hat a bit lower over his eyes to hide the twinkle. "I didn't say that. I said I didn't want a wife." It didn't take much to put this woman on the attack. He'd have to remember that.

"Then you do have a…" She stopped abruptly and folded her face into a thoughtful expression.

J.D. let her stew for a minute, rather flattered by her interest in his love life, which was relatively tame. He discovered steady girlfriends had too many expectations. Then he realized Rebecca's interest was probably directed toward whether or not he could be an appropriate "parent" for Jessie if his sister didn't show up. He hooked his thumbs into his belt, deciding to jump into the subject that had been on his mind since early this morning. "I've been thinking. I don't think it is too advisable for you and the baby to stay here. There's a nice, little motel in town where you'd be more comfortable."

"In town? I didn't see a town on my way here."

"That's 'cause the town is the opposite direction from the way you came to the ranch. If you came from the nearest airport, that is." He held up a hand, acknowledging, "Now, granted, Wildwalk isn't much of a place, but there's a motel that can find room for the two of you for a couple of weeks. You'd be a lot more comfortable there than out here on the ranch with me…doing without any of the things you'd probably call home. At least Wildwalk has sidewalks, and a picture show—"

"Why don't you want us here?"

Faced with such a bald question, J.D. wasn't sure he had an answer. He just felt, deep down in his gut, that having the two of them living with him wasn't a good idea, above and beyond what would be best for the baby, that is. But as he was used to having his statements obeyed, not questioned, he decided to ignore her, saying instead, "It would just be better if you were in Wildwalk."

"Better for whom? Surely not the baby?"

"Better for both of you."

No, that's not right. It's better for me, he thought, as he looked away from her persistent gaze. It's better that the sight of her and that baby didn't lead him to imagining things better left alone. J.D. set out to convince her. "You could use another woman around to gossip with and go to for advice. And Edna Mae runs the motel. She's a woman." Of course, he wasn't going to mention that Edna Mae was the same age as Smoke, and a spinster who'd probably never cared for a baby in her life. She was still a woman, and that's what mattered to J.D.'s way of thinking.

"That's what you think I need—gossip, advice and sidewalks?"

He shifted his weight suddenly. She was so indignant that J.D. almost grinned, but he managed to keep it back. "Well, you're going to be pretty lonely here with me out and about all day working the ranch and Smoke busy as hell, too." He wondered if his excuses sounded as transparent to her as they sounded to him.

Rebecca walked over to join him at the corral. "Don't you worry about me. I'll find something to do. Besides, taking care of a baby is going to fill up my time. So, it won't be a problem." She sent him a challenging look and placed her hands on her hips. "Now that you don't have to concern yourself with that, there's no need to mention the motel again. I'm sure I can survive the lack of a city for two weeks. And so can Jessie."

J.D. wasn't so sure. However, her clenched jaw made it very clear that short of tossing her in the back of his pickup truck, there was no way he'd get her to go. He decided he might as well make the best of things. Time enough to take a stand when she came to her senses and realized that Rosalie would disappoint her, too. He hoped he'd have the stamina to pick her up and help her go on when it happened. He'd hate to see the bitter disappointment creep into Rebecca's eyes the way it had crept into his.

Rebecca allowed a small smile to peep out at him as she stated, "Now, aren't you glad that's settled?"

J.D. said nothing, hoping he looked like the trademark laconic cowboy, instead of a man whose emotions were churning until they could have made butter.

After a moment, Rebecca turned away from him and looked out over the corral to the rolling hills beyond. She took a deep breath. "Smoke sent me out here to see what Texas looks like in the morning."

Relieved to change the subject, J.D. turned and leaned his forearms on the top railing. "It looks like heaven, of course." Or was that the woman next to him?

Rebecca smiled, and slid him a look from under her lashes. "Oh, of course."

J.D. knew he was licked for the moment, so he gave in with good grace. Deliberately he relaxed his muscles and teased, "You've gotta understand, Reb, there are two types of people in this world. Texans—" he grinned "—and everyone else."

She leaned her elbow on the railing and cupped her cheek in her palm as she regarded him. "I see."

"Now, the way I figure it. God really knew what he was doing when he made Texas. He gave us all the space we could ever need on the ground and all the blue sky we could ever look at up above." He wondered if someone like Rebecca could ever learn to appreciate it. Then he mentally kicked himself—what did it matter?

Laughing, Rebecca played along. "And on the seventh day He rested, I suppose?"

J.D. laughed back at her as he swept his arm out to indicate the landscape. "Wouldn't you?"

"Well, it sure is big. I'll go along with that."

"It's gotta be big to contain a Texan."

"Like you, you mean?"

J.D. winked and agreed. He recognized the curiosity underscoring the teasing. Suddenly, he wanted her to understand why this place meant so much to him. "Like me, and my daddy, and my granddaddy, and the one before him even. We've all been here since the beginning and I reckon we'll all die here. That's the way it is for the McCoys." That's why he couldn't risk introducing this baby to what the ranch meant to the family. He didn't want Jessie to stay here, to foster false hopes. Especially as every instinct screamed that if her mother did show up someday, she'd just take her away again.

"Oh, really."

"Yep. McCoys plant their roots deep."

"They do, huh?" Rebecca was enjoying J.D.'s relaxed banter so much that she was tempted to continue flirting with him in the Texas sunshine. The powerful sight of J.D. suddenly relaxed and amused, she discovered, almost took her breath away. But first, she had a job to do. Rebecca needed to know one thing. The one thing that had been haunting her since yesterday.

"Then why did Rosalie leave?"

5

The stench of failure stung his nostrils as her question slammed into his gut. J.D. wasn't sure how to answer her for a moment, then he decided he had to tell her the whole truth. So she would understand why Rosalie had left, and why she'd never come back. It would help prepare Rebecca for the inevitable—taking the baby to a home where she'd be better off in the long run. Perhaps it would help him, too to guard against the hope that had leaped into his heart since Rebecca and that little girl arrived last night. From that sly little dream of having a family of his own that had slipped into his mind when he let his guard down.

"You have to understand that Rosalie was always one for drama, for making the big gesture. She was like my mama in that respect. That's why my sister does some of the things she does."

"Like leaving the baby on my doorstep?"

J.D. nodded. "It fits her. To understand my sister you have to go a long way back. You see, our daddy died when Rosalie was about eight. That was hard. That little girl sure loved her daddy. From that point on, I filled in as best I could. I was the man in the family for Rosalie, Mama—" he gestured at the sweeping landscape before him "—and I took care of the spread."

"How did your father die?"

"He got pneumonia. We were real shorthanded one year

and he kept pushing and pushing himself to get the stock in and do all the work. I was finishing up my last year of high school and—'' Lord, he hated remembering this ''—I wasn't as much help as I could have been. Anyway, he got sick and just kept working. Before we knew how bad it was, he was gone.''

''Oh, how awful.''

J.D. shrugged and glanced at Rebecca. ''God's will, I suppose. Even with that tragedy, though, we stayed real strong as a family. Me, Mom and Rosalie. My mama was one tough lady. A real Texan, if you know what I mean.''

Rebecca lifted her shoulders, almost apologetically. ''Well, no, I don't.''

''Mom was tough enough to handle most things…the sort of woman who followed the road west, in other words. Soft and tender, but strong and determined. The kind of woman the west depends on to support its menfolk.'' He glanced at Rebecca, surprised to see a faint look of unease pass over her face. He wondered why.

''Anyway, after Dad died, Rosalie got really attached to Mama. When she wasn't sticking close to our mother she was following me. I guess that's why it hit her so hard.''

Brow wrinkled and ready to listen, Rebecca settled her shoulder more comfortably against the railing. ''What did?''

''Mom's accident.''

''Rosalie didn't mention an accident.''

''I'm not surprised.'' J.D. looked at the ranch house, re-membering, ''Just before Dad died he spent most of our ready cash on a good stallion and mare. He intended to raise a prime herd of horses. After he died, those horses were my responsibility. We had a young horse I'd just bro-ken to saddle and one day my Mom decided to finish the job.''

''Your mother was breaking horses?''

He grinned at the horror in her voice. ''My mother had

been on horseback since before she could walk—she was practically a bronco buster. Dad met her at a rodeo. She was a barrel racer then.'' At her look of disbelief, J.D. couldn't help probing, ''Do you ride?''

''The only type of Bronco I ride is made in Detroit.''

J.D. couldn't help but chuckle. It was easier than concentrating on the story he was telling. He lifted his Stetson, rubbed his forehead and replaced the hat. He knew he needed to get this over with, so he rushed to get it out. ''I was out fixing fences when it happened or I would have stopped her. Smoke said Mom decided to take that horse out for a run and really let her rip. There were times when my mama had more nerve than sense.''

Rebecca half smiled. ''She sounds something like her daughter.''

The truth of that slammed J.D. again. That knowledge should have guided his actions when it came to handling Rosalie. Unfortunately, it didn't always. Generally she'd push him until he lost his temper and then his reason went out the window. He turned and faced the coral, looking out over it toward the landscape beyond. He laced his fingers together, gesturing toward the fields with his folded hands. ''That horse stepped in a hole out there, and went down. My mother sailed over her neck and…''

From the corner of his eye, he saw Rebecca reach as if to touch his arm, but she stopped as he flinched from her. He couldn't help pulling back. He'd got through the pain by burying it under everyday activities after the accident happened. Now withdrawing had become a habit. Even if he wanted to break it, he wasn't sure he could.

Rebecca withdrew her hand and gripped the railing instead. ''J.D., I'm sorry.''

The sympathy in her voice rained on his heart like a soft spring shower, but he held himself tight. He couldn't give in to the pain. The pain he still felt for the parents who had meant everything to him, the parents who had worked so hard for the ranch he was standing on. "Rosalie came home from school later that day and found the ranch shut down and quiet. Smoke was waiting for her, 'cause I'd gone to the hospital."

"How old was Rosalie?"

"Thirteen."

"That's a difficult age for girls, anyway. For Rosalie to lose her mother on top of that…"

J.D. gave her a look. "That's the truth. Hell, I was only twenty-three myself."

Rebecca risked placing her hand on his arm then and he accepted it for a moment, letting her strong warmth creep into his clenched muscles. He wasn't sure why, but he had a feeling this woman understood pain. After a moment, he shrugged. "It's water over the dam. Anyway, I had to take over everything—the ranch, the stock, my parent's dreams and raising Rosalie."

"It must have been very difficult. I'll bet she was an emotional mess, wasn't she?"

He shook his head. "Not so you'd notice on the outside. She kept it all inside after Mom died. She never even referred to that day, even though I tried to get her to talk about it. Rosalie just got more and more brittle…and wild. She started sneaking off at night, to meet her boyfriend, I thought. So I laid down the law and she started defying me. Started telling me that she hated me, and hated the ranch."

Rebecca murmured, "That would be typical behavior under the circumstances."

After a brief glance at Rebecca, J.D. adjusted his hat, pulling it lower over his forehead to put some cover between his expression and the woman next to him. He stared at the barn and continued, determined to get everything out once and for all. Then he wouldn't discuss it again—ever. He'd put it back in his heart where it belonged. "Finally, she didn't muck out the stalls one day. That was one of her jobs, the stalls.''

''The horses? After—''

J.D. waved his hand. ''I know what you're gonna say. At first I tried to keep her away from the horses. Then she told me to stop being such a mother hen. She knew our horses were the cornerstone of our future success.''

''Still—''

''Anyway, that day I lit into her for not cleaning the stalls. Told her I didn't have time to do it, what with trying to be father, mother, ranch hand—you get the picture. Finally she told me I wouldn't have to worry about it anymore. That she hated the ranch and she hated me. She was going to take herself off to the big city, so she could live her life like a real person instead of a two-bit cowgirl. She said she didn't care if she ever saw the ranch again.'' He gripped his fingers until he could see the knuckles whiten, then made himself relax so she wouldn't notice. The memory still drove a nail though J.D.'s heart at the way she'd denied the ranch he'd given up his life for.

''I just thought it was talk. But Rosalie left in the middle of the night. Ran away with her high school boyfriend and I never did hear from her again.''

''That's not what she—''

''So you see, Rebecca—'' J.D. turned to face her ''—when you say Rosalie is coming back here, I have to say—you're dreaming, lady.''

''I understand.'' Rebecca was quiet for a long moment. Then she angled to look at him directly. ''Why didn't you try to find her, J.D.?''

''I did. But I didn't have a lot of spare money under the circumstances. Oh, I contacted all the authorities, even managed to get a private eye for a while. Until I couldn't afford to pay him anymore. At one point, her boyfriend sent a postcard to his parents from L.A. and they called to tell me. I managed to get there in time to see her dust.''

"Do you think he's the father?"

"I thought they'd split up. Last I heard from his parents, he's in Wyoming. Later, I got some information from a college friend of mine who thought she'd seen Rosalie in Chicago. Then nothing." He rubbed his forehead. "Just another runaway statistic."

"A young woman without roots. I can relate. My mother and I managed to see a lot of the East Coast before we ended up in Boston. The old homestead and the people in it were constantly changing, you see."

He was caught by the bitterness in her voice, but before he could comment on it, Rebecca folded back into her professional self and gave him a kind smile saying, "Unlike most of you McCoys."

It was the kind of practiced smile J.D. imagined her using on the people she worked with. He didn't like being slotted into that category. It made him want to ruffle her feathers to see some of that fire she had banked down again. He'd have to work on that. Now wasn't the time, though.

"Most McCoys but Rosalie, you mean?" Unexpectedly, he found himself grinning, "Somehow, Reb, I can't see my wildcat sister in Boston, among all those uptight Yankees."

Rebecca grinned back. "You'd be surprised what those uptight Yankees are up to in Boston."

Nodding, J.D. removed his foot from the railing and readjusted his hat so he could take a good look at her. "Is that so?" He deliberately tried to lighten the moment. He'd had enough melodrama to last him a lifetime.

She straightened, her fingers worrying her neckline. "Well, some of them anyway."

He lifted a brow, thinking she looked soft and appealing, with her eyes big and concerned and her mouth relaxed into a smile, a real one this time. Not like a stiff Yankee at all. He took a moment to enjoy himself. He figured he deserved it. "And you, Reb? What have you been up to?"

Rebecca backed away as his gaze dropped to her mouth.

"Well, I…um…I should go in and see how Smoke is doing with Jessie."

That brought him back to earth. Hooking his thumbs in his belt, he replied, "That's a good idea. 'Cause Smoke's heart was broken when Rosalie left. I wouldn't want to see him get too attached to the baby."

"What about you, J.D.?"

J.D. didn't want to get attached to her, either. But he didn't say it aloud. Instead, he walked over to pick up his mug and handed it to Rebecca. Not answering seemed to be answer enough. After a moment, she turned on her heel and walked slowly to the house.

"Rebecca," J.D. called, unable to let her go for some reason. "Since you refuse to leave, I'll get up to the attic this afternoon and track down the old baby stuff, okay? That'll make it a bit easier on you."

She looked over her shoulder and smiled. "Thanks. That'll be helpful."

"I'd do it now, but I have to go out and round up my cattle. I'm still missing a few."

"Oh, sure, I understand. Don't worry about us, J.D. I might not be a *Texas woman,* but I'm still pretty tough." With a little wave, she walked to the house and went inside.

J.D. chuckled over her last comment as he watched her go. She headed toward the rear of the house. He smiled, thinking how good it felt to see a woman using the back door like she belonged there. He'd missed that. Then he pulled himself up short. *Idiot! As if a woman like Rebecca Chandler could ever belong in a place like this.* J.D. whistled for his dog and headed to the corral to saddle his horse.

Rebecca stopped just inside the covered porch, almost overwhelmed with the tale she'd just heard. *Lord, what have I gotten myself into?* She had no inkling of what to do about this situation. She was a professional, for God's sake, but she sure hadn't acted like one with the McCoy family. If she'd had any idea—! Yet she should have, the

way Rosalie had avoided some of her questions, preferring
to speak about innocuous memories instead. Rebecca could
kick herself for not probing more deeply, for being so
charmed by the girl and her baby that she neglected her
real responsibilities. Rebecca buried her face in her hands.
J.D. could be right. Rosalie might not come back.

But she'd sent her baby—surely that meant something?
Didn't that mean that she truly believed the child would be
better off with her brother than with her? Rebecca lifted
her head and focused on the interior door into the kitchen.
Was that what Rosalie had been saying to her all along?
Only Rebecca had stupidly turned it into a crusade to save
a family...to help create a tidy little family unit for Rosalie
and Jessie. And if that was what she'd done—what did it
say about her judgment? How could she trust herself from
now on if even her desire to keep this small family together
was suspect? Was it for Rosalie's sake that she wanted to
do so, or for her own? For the first time Rebecca wondered
if she'd used this situation as a substitute for her own lack
of a strong family when she was growing up. Maybe since
she hadn't been able to do anything about her mother's
many marriages, she hoped she could do something about
this.

Rebecca paced across the slanted floorboards, up to the
washer and dryer and then back to the storage shelves just
inside the door. *What now? Should I take J.D.'s suggestion
and stay in a motel until I make a decision? Or go back to
Boston and confess the entire incident to my boss and hope
he'll understand?* That latter was probably the right thing
to do. But what was right for Jessie? For that little girl who
had a whole life stretching out before her?

Call her a fool, but a spark of belief still burned inside,
telling Rebecca that what was right for the youngest McCoy
was to stay right here on the ranch. To learn about the land,
her land, from a man who loved it. To learn about her
heritage from a man who lived it. To learn about love from

a man who'd lost it and, she thought, still longed for it. And finally, to learn about hope from a man who existed on it—whether he admitted it or not. With a decisive nod, Rebecca concluded that Jessie needed to stay right here. Now the problem was convincing J.D. She could only hope Smoke had been right when he told her that J.D. knew his niece really belonged here. It would make her job a lot easier. Thinking back, she thought she'd seen a bit of relief when J.D. agreed they should stay on the ranch.

She have to do a lot more thinking about how to proceed—but not now.

Baby noises from the other side of the door told her she needed to take care of Jessie. Rebecca turned the knob and stepped through the doorway into the kitchen. She walked inside, only to find Jessie was not unhappy at all. She was squealing, babbling and happily kicking her feet as she sat in her infant seat. Smoke had placed it in the middle of the table facing him. He was sitting at the far end of the table, nursing his mug of coffee as he sat turning the pages of a dog-eared journal.

The air smelled a bit better now. Probably because Smoke had capped a lid on his cooking pot and turned on the ceiling fan. A slight breeze circulated as the blades turned lazily, with a soft, relaxing hum...so welcome after the heat and tension outside. She could feel her shoulders start to relax.

Rebecca glanced from the baby to Smoke. "Did Jessie eat her breakfast?"

The old cowhand dragged his eyes from the ragged pages to look up at her. "She's stuffed as full as a piglet with a full trough of slop."

"I beg your pardon?" Rebecca's brows lifted as she tried to picture the image.

"She's full-up, that's all I meant." Chuckling, Smoke pushed away from the table. He wrinkled his nose until it resembled an accordion. "So full she overflowed."

"Oh."

"Glad you're back." He put some distance between himself and the table. "I took care of one end of this young'un, but you gotta take care of the other."

"The other?" As Rebecca stepped closer, she caught a faint whiff of the real reason Smoke had probably turned on the fan—not the pig food, but the baby. "Ohhh! Change her diaper, you mean?"

"That's right. I'll shovel it in, but I ain't shoveling it out for nobody."

Rebecca laughed. "I don't blame you." She glanced at Jessie. "Although she doesn't seem too distressed by it, does she?"

"It ain't her I'm concerned with," Smoke said with a dry expression as he walked to the sink.

"I'll be out in the garden. I got things to do and no time to waste."

Rebecca started to lift the baby seat, stopping to say, "Smoke, can I help you? Maybe I could straighten up and dust a bit."

Smoke sent her a funny look. "Dust?" His lips pursed around the syllable as if he'd never tasted the word.

"Dust," she said firmly. "Getting the layers of dirt off all the standing surfaces, like the table in the hallway, the stairs, the—"

"We-ll," Smoke drawled, "if you wanna waste your time doin' what's gonna happen all over again tomorrow, I guess I ain't one to stop ya. Don't know how J.D. will feel about it, though." He jerked his head, indicating the porch. "You'll find some rags out there. Might even be some lemon oil or something, too. Help yourself."

"I'll change Jessie, then get started." With the baby carrier in her arms, Rebecca left the kitchen. She walked slowly through the hallway, peering into the rooms to either side, trying to decide where to start. She peeked through an archway into the long living room that ran the full length of the house. "We'll start in here. Okay, Jessie?"

The only answer Jessie gave her was a nonverbal one. With total concentration, she scrunched up her little face until it turned bright red—almost managing to cross her eyes in the process—and grunted. Rebecca wrinkled her nose and held her at arm's length.

"Whew! Are you sure Smoke didn't feed you his pig food instead of your baby cereal?" Rebecca whirled away from the living room and dashed for the steps, anxious to change this baby as fast as possible. "We'll get started down here after we make you presentable for polite society. It's a good thing your uncle's not around. He sure wouldn't find you very appealing at the moment."

As she dashed upstairs, Rebecca suddenly realized she had the answer to her dilemma. She'd have to make Jessie an integral part of J.D.'s life. So much so that, regardless of what happened with his sister, he wouldn't consider giving this baby away to anyone else. Somehow she'd have to involve J.D. in everything concerning this child during the next two weeks, because she truly believed Jessie belonged in Texas.

Rebecca grabbed a fresh diaper and baby wipes from the bag in her room, then headed to the bathroom where she powdered and rediapered Jessie, and changed her one-piece cover-up to a little sunsuit with a duck on the front. "There you go. From now on, we want your Uncle J.D. to see just how adorable you are. You're going to be adorable every minute, aren't you, Jessie?" In response, Jessie waved her arms, kicked her legs and grinned, a big, happy, slobbery grin. Then, as Rebecca pulled her to a sitting position, Jessie burped and spit up all over her new clean clothes.

"Oh, dear…" Rebecca bit her lip as she looked down at the soiled baby. "This might be a bit tougher than I thought."

* * *

Rebecca spent the rest of the morning trying to put the living room into some semblance of cleanliness and order. She'd discovered that trying to get anything done with a baby who also wanted some attention was almost impossible. Finally Rebecca put her dusting cloth and polish on the living room mantelpiece and walked over to Jessie, who was fussing and kicking mightily in her baby seat.

"I'm sorry, sweetheart. Are you bored?" Rebecca bent over and undid the safety restraints. "Here, let's get you out of there." The minute she lifted the baby from the seat, Jessie started to smile and gurgle. "You just want some attention don't you? You want to play." Holding the baby close, Rebecca started to sing a silly tune and whirl in a circle. Within a few minutes, Jessie was laughing...big baby chuckles that made Rebecca laugh in response.

"I haven't heard that sound in this house for quite a while."

Rebecca stumbled to a stop near the doorway and turned to look over her shoulder. She studied the dusty man standing in the arch. She caught her breath at the expression in his eyes—warm, admiring and...something deeper. Regret? Perhaps for the laughter that had disappeared with his family, or for the lack of a child's laughter? After all, he had practically raised his sister. Whatever the reason, the regret made a stronger impact on Rebecca than the admiration. Wanting to chase the sadness from his face, she grinned. "Are you talking about my singing?"

J.D.'s eyes lightened as he grinned back. He flicked a thumb under the brim of his hat and cocked it to the back of his head, leaving a shock of sun-streaked hair free to flop over his forehead. "Oh, is that what that was?"

"From your reaction I guess I'd better keep my day job?"

"Rebecca, let's just say the last time I heard a voice like that, it was laying time in the henhouse."

Rebecca shifted Jessie around, so she could clasp her

chest dramatically with her other hand. "Wounded. A blow to the heart." From her new position, Jessie now got a good look at J.D. as he stood nearby. Abruptly the baby let out a delighted squeal and leaned over, spreading her arms wide so J.D. could take her. "Oh, isn't this cute? She wants to go to you, J.D."

Amazed, J.D. stood and looked at them for a second. "Why?"

Rebecca laughed. "I guess she likes you." Rebecca stepped a bit closer and turned to allow the baby to reach again toward her uncle. Without giving J.D. an opportunity to refuse, she said, "Here you go, Uncle J.D." Smoothly she transferred the grinning baby from her arms to the male arms that had reluctantly come up to take the squirming infant.

To Rebecca, J.D. looked as if he'd just been handed a live grenade. Once again, Rebecca wanted to tell him to go with it…just let the moment happen. But she could appreciate the irony of her giving that type of advice to him. She, who allowed no moment to creep up on her without an appointment, was a fine one to be giving insights on spontaneity. Unfortunately, as that was her role at the moment, she had to play it as best she could. "Relax, J.D. She wants to play. Hang on to her though, she's getting pretty strong."

Hesitantly, he pulled her a bit closer. However, his reluctance to get close was not shared by his niece. With a happy screech, that probably registered high enough on the decibel level to break glass, Jessie managed to anchor her bare toes against his belt and straighten her legs so she stood up in his arms to look him straight in the eye. She grinned, then immediately reached forward and grabbed a big hunk of J.D.'s hair, then followed with the same action on the other side. Now, the one thing holding her upright, besides J.D.'s strong arms, was her grasp on the sun-bleached thatch that framed his tanned face. With another ear-shattering squeal, Jessie yanked on his hair, then bended her knees and dug her toes into his belly to bounce up and yank it again.

"Ouch! That's not a bale of hay. That hurts."

Jessie chuckled, twisted her fingers for a better grip and leaned forward, toward J.D.'s face. Her mouth opened wide and she went straight for his nose. Startled, J.D. tried to twist away, but was unable to do so before the baby managed to hit her target and slobber all over the side of his nose and cheek. "Hey."

Rebecca clapped her hands. "Oh, that's so sweet!"

"Sweet!" J.D. reared back to look sideways around the baby's head at Rebecca. "She's trying to eat me alive. Don't you feed this kid?"

"She's giving you a kiss, J.D. That's how she does it." Rebecca could scarcely control her amusement at the sight of the big, tall Texan standing statue-still because an eighteen-pound infant had gotten the best of him. It was a sight Rebecca vowed to remember, as she'd bet a month's salary that no one got the best of J. D. McCoy very often.

Jessie released one of her fists from J.D.'s hair and accidentally clunked him on the cheekbone. She lifted her face and gave him a saucy look, her long lashes sweeping down flirtatiously. "Ooo-aahh."

J.D. couldn't keep the smile off his lips as he looked Jessie straight in the eye. "Oh, you think so, do you? You little hussy. What do you think you're doing, running around kissing strange men? Don't think I'll let you get away with that behavior when you get older, 'cause I won't, young lady."

Rebecca held her breath as she watched them and listened to J.D.'s unconscious response to the baby in his arms. Did he realize what he was saying? Realize he was moving one step closer to accepting his niece's presence in his life? His gaze suddenly met hers. She tried to keep her triumphant thoughts from her expression, but wasn't sure she managed it. She was positive she hadn't when J.D.'s relaxed expression suddenly started to freeze over. Within moments it went from easy charm to a careful politeness.

"Here, Reb. You'd better take her." J.D. detached the baby and gently dumped her into Rebecca's arms. "I just came inside to clean up a bit so I could find that crib and put it together for you before the baby's nap time."

Rebecca rocked Jessie in her arms. "Oh, thanks. That's very thoughtful."

J.D.'s gaze lingered for a moment on Jessie now happily trying to grab her toes while she rested snugly cradled in Rebecca's arms. "I'll…um…" He backed toward the hall and jerked his thumb over his shoulder. "I'll be up in the attic."

Rebecca followed him out into the hall. "Do you need any help?"

He muttered something that Rebecca didn't quite catch. For a moment it sounded like "All I can get." Before she could comment though, he shook his head.

"Nah…I'll manage."

"I can hold the sides of the bed so you can put them together more easily, J.D. That way I can get Jessie down for her nap sooner." Looking down at the alert, round-eyed baby in her arms, Rebecca played her trump card. "I think she's starting to get sleepy." Hopefully, Jessie would eventually cooperate and not make a liar out of her, she thought.

Rebecca hoped that comment about his niece would change his mind, would allow some of the reserve he'd summoned when he felt himself softening toward the infant to recede. But that wasn't the only reason. If she was really honest, she'd admit she didn't want him to walk away from her. Moments before, she'd had a true glimpse of the type of father he might make and it was devastating. The glimpse provoked strange feelings. A longing to be the other point of the triangle…the irresistible triangle of love that moved eternally from mother to father to baby. Re-

becca waited, praying he'd agree, unwilling to continue an-
alyzing why it was so important to her. The air around her
suddenly stilled, as if nature understood the impact his next
comment would have.

J.D. hesitated, then said quietly. "I can use some help,
I guess."

Slowly, Rebecca exhaled. With this self-sufficient man
that statement might have indicated only a tiny crack in his
armor, but time would take care of that. Time would allow
that crack to widen, much the way water carved deep can-
yons in the mountains...one drop at a time. Watching J.D.
climb the stairs and disappear into the upstairs hallway,
Rebecca suddenly wished she could be here for the entire
erosion, instead of the preliminary event.

After all, what was waiting for her in Boston? Each day
she worked overtime, then stopped at the health food store
and deli on the way home because she was too tired to
cook. If she had the energy she'd take a trip to the spa,
then make a quick stop at the video store or bookshop down
the block from her apartment. Then she tucked herself in
for the night. That is, if her mother didn't have some society event that demanded her presence. Or some new, perfectly bred, perfectly dressed, perfectly...boring man for
her to meet. Fortunately, Rebecca had gotten much better
at getting out of both of those situations over the past year.
Currently, most nights ended with her alone, curled up on
her sofa.

As she climbed the stairs after J.D., Rebecca pondered
how funny it was that an evening in an old ranch house
plunked in the middle of nowhere suddenly seemed so
much more appealing. Glimpsing J.D. opening the attic
door at the far end of the hallway, and watching the action
of his trim buttocks as he climbed the narrow stairs con-
firmed her opinion.

Definitely more appealing!

6

After lunch Rebecca put Jessie down for a nap in the crib that had once held her mother, then she went back to the living room to finish cleaning. An hour and a half later, she looked around satisfied that she'd taken one more step toward making J.D.'s house feel like a home. Contented, she stared at the creamy walls glowing with light, at the dark, comfortable furniture and wide-planked floor, gleaming with friendliness. For a moment she closed her eyes and dreamed this was her house. She dreamed she belonged. Belonged in this room, with this lived-in feeling that could only have come from many generations of use. For the first time in her life, she dreamed of an actual place where her roots could grow instead of being continually replanted. A place where she could flourish. Like his mother had, and the women before... Rebecca opened her eyes. She stood still and let the heat of reality beat against her until she forced herself to acknowledge the truth.

How arrogant for her to dream she belonged here, Rebecca thought, to briefly imagine she could stand alongside the women in his family. How did one end up the type of woman who tamed the West and the men in it? The type like J.D.'s mother, who dealt effortlessly with disaster, her house, her ranch and her children. How could another woman live up to a legend that huge? Rebecca sure couldn't.

Regardless of how she proclaimed herself a modern, liberated woman, she was having trouble taming her own life, much less the lives of the people involved in it. Look at the mess she'd made so far. Twenty-eight years old and nothing to show for it. No family, no roots to anchor her to the earth, no lasting accomplishments. Instead she had a tense intestine, occasional headaches and a vague ache where satisfaction should be.

Coming to Texas had started a longing within her that she didn't understand. She only hoped she would find a way to deal with it before she left.

Unable to relax, she looked around for something else to concentrate on. There, at the far end of the room, near the double doors that opened onto the garden area, she found it. J.D.'s desk. A heavily carved oak desk with an overwhelming leather chair behind it. Directly behind the chair stood old wooden file cabinets. The file drawers were half closed but folders protruded from the gaping openings. Other files and books were stacked haphazardly on top of the cabinets. But that didn't come close to the mess the desk contained. However, Rebecca had taken on tougher challenges than this. Taking a firmer grip on her dust cloth and polish, she advanced on the desk, hands poised and ready for battle.

After a half hour of solid work, Rebecca finally had everything organized. As she placed the last stack of files on the top of the drawers, she realized she'd neglected to clean the top of the cabinets. She pushed the rolling leather chair against the files and stood on it, carefully stretching to reach the very back of the cabinets with her dusting cloth. Poised precariously, Rebecca lifted to her tiptoes and reached to swipe at a particularly annoying spider web.

"What the hell do you think you're doing?"

Startled by the roar over her right shoulder, Rebecca jumped. She lurched to the right as the chair rolled to the left. Trying to find something to hold on to, her hand swiped the stack of files and knocked it off the top of the cabinets. Just as she was about to test the appeal of the newly waxed floor for herself, strong arms snatched her around the waist. She continued to fall, but J.D. must have rolled to take the brunt of their weight. All Rebecca knew was the floor was a lot softer than she'd expected.

After first enjoying the sheer sensation of being clamped against 175 pounds of sheer grit and muscle, she came to her senses. Tentatively she stretched, realizing that the rock-hard body she was laying on top of might not be any softer than the floor, but it was a hell of a lot more comfortable—if the darting impulses that were short-circuiting her nervous system could be called comfortable. Heaven knows they were certainly the most vivid vibes she'd felt in a long time.

His hands raced over her, patting and soothing. ''Are you hurt, Reb?''

Rebecca looked down into the concerned eyes about an inch from her own and melted against him. He felt like home. ''Hurt? Oh no. I'm lovely thank you. How are you?''

She could see how he was. The unease that still shadowed his eyes from their earlier encounters remained. Obviously dredging up old memories had been devastating. Something Rebecca completely understood. He seemed to conduct his life much as she did, by burying himself in his work to avoid dealing with his personal issues. But she was too comfortable to probe any more, so she merely tightened her grasp on his arms.

''I'm lovely too, thanks.'' J.D.'s beautiful mouth wavered as he tried to suppress a grin.

Rebecca found it amazing to watch. She wanted to taste that mouth. For the first time in her life she wanted to throw caution aside, let down her guard and feel. She wanted to kiss away the vulnerability and self-blame she'd seen on that mouth earlier, out by the barn and later as he automatically assembled Jessie's new bed in his runaway sister's former room. Rebecca wanted to kiss those hurts away almost as much as she wanted to share his present humor and appetite for life. Unable to stop herself, Rebecca lowered her lips to his and pressed them softly against those firm lips. She felt his smile fade into something else... something focused, something intense, something unexpected, something dangerous—so dangerous. She shivered as J.D.'s lips started to nibble hers, taking tiny nips that he turned into a kiss as long, as slow, as hot as the Texas afternoon. Rebecca could feel everything heating. Who said she didn't like the heat? If this was what Texas heat was really like she could stay here until her well dried up! Judging by the liquid condition of her insides, that would be a long, long time coming.

When his tongue moved to touch hers, then tangle, Rebecca went wild. She plunged her fingers into his hair, enjoying the long strands that slipped through her fingers like warm ribbons. She tugged to bring him even closer to her. Then she was stunned when his hands slipped down her back to cup her buttocks and press her against him. Her hips rocked forward to meet his hard masculinity. Where there was heat, there was now steam. Rebecca suddenly realized she would do anything to have this man make love to her, to slide his fingers under her clothes and— With that realization she panicked.

What on earth am I doing?

Gasping, she tore her lips from his. Pressing a hand against his chest, she lifted her head so she could breathe. Air rushed into her lungs. She'd never done anything this spontaneous before—except for her blinding dash to Texas with an abandoned baby. Feeling the heat rush into her cheeks and hit the tip of her nose, she tried to make light of the situation. She didn't know what else to do. "Well...thanks for the rescue."

"My pleasure."

Although he didn't give it voice, she felt his chuckle as

it rippled along her body, which was still intimately pressed to his. The heat of his body reflected the embarrassed heat now rising in her face. Yet, his understated humor and the ease with which he accepted the situation attracted her so much that she tried to scramble off him in self-defense. He clamped his arm around her waist to keep her in place.

What was the matter with her? How could she mistake the man on the floor with the stability and permanence she'd always longed for? A man who'd closed himself off from involvement, from family? How could she let herself be so tempted? J. D. McCoy was a stranger, with a life-style that was totally foreign. A life-style she could never embrace, even as it wove a seductive spell around her. Or was he the one weaving the spell? At that realization, Rebecca tried once again to push herself away. She couldn't stop the alarm in her voice as she said the first thing that popped into her mind, ''I can't believe I'm lying on the floor kissing a man I only met a day ago. A man wearing spurs of all things. This wouldn't happen in Boston.''

Rebecca felt his body stiffen. What had been pliable and so molded to hers that she'd been unable to tell them apart, now became as tough and inflexible as old shoe leather. Finally he said, ''Well, don't hold back. For a casual acquaintance, how'd I do?'' Then he really let go and started to wind himself up. ''Did I match up with all those sophisticated dudes you're used to falling on top of back east? And I'm sorry if my spurs bother you, but don't you worry, Reb, 'cause a cowboy only needs 'em to control his horse…not his women. We have better ways of doing that.''

He certainly did. She'd just had a taste. At the moment, Rebecca was mortified to think how easily he could control her if he really made an effort. It terrified her to realize how close he'd come; and how close she'd come to letting him. She panicked and to protect herself, deliberately set out to encourage his hurt and misunderstanding with the only thing she could think of. She tried to reduce him to a stereotype, to the very Westerner that she'd thought to find when she'd first come to Texas, and had been shocked to discover did not exist. "You compared very well, J.D. Now I understand why women always fall for Western men in books and movies. There's something so romantic about it...this whole mystique of the iron-jawed cowboy. Not at all taciturn or dull—"

"No more compliments, please. I don't think I could take them. Just consider that kiss another taste of Texas hospitality, Miss Chandler. You let me know anytime ya'll want a repeat, ya hear?"

Right then, as the hard, sardonic drawl of his voice pelted her, Rebecca knew she'd made a royal mess of the situation. How could she be so stupid? Just because she was completely disconcerted by her reaction to him was no reason for her to practically call him a cartoon character, or worse, indicate he was a common two-dimensional cardboard cowboy cutout! She knew it wasn't true, that was part of the problem. Ashamed, she tried to apologize. "J.D., I'm sorry. I didn't mean that...."

He levered her away from him and placed her effortlessly to the side. Like a tumbleweed that annoyed him. "Glad I could be of help, ma'am. Now if you'll forgive me for saying so, I'd appreciate it if you'd keep your lovely little hands off my private...papers. I've given you permission to stay for a while, not take over my entire life."

"I was just straightening up a bit. I don't understand how you can run a business—" With each sentence she uttered to try to normalize the situation in her mind, she could feel his ferocity increase. With a flash of morbid humor Rebecca realized she'd be better off pulling her foot out of her mouth and throwing herself at his feet so he could step on her...grind her under his heel like a nasty bug.

J.D. rose to his full height and looked down. "Tell you what, Rebecca. Why don't you stick to watching the baby, and I'll stick to watching the ranch. Just as I've been doing most of my life. That way we should get along fine.'' Without another word he moved around to the other side of the desk to start picking up his files.

A headache started to pound behind her eyes. ''J.D., I didn't mean to—''

''The baby's crying.''

His flat tone made it very clear that from now on, her place in the household had been relegated to childcare—only. No more sharing, no more moving toward a new level of understanding. Rebecca stared at his rigid back for a moment as Jessie's crying echoed down the stairway. Although she knew she deserved his anger for her thoughtless behavior, she couldn't accept it. She indicated the mess on the floor. ''I'll be right back to help you clean—''

''There's no need. I don't need any more help.'' He bent over to pick up some files. ''I've been helping myself for a long time now.''

''But it was my fault. I—''

''Forget it, Rebecca.'' His voice turned soft and husky, as if he couldn't keep his emotions under wraps any longer. ''The damage is already done.''

J.D. was right. The damage was done all right! One kiss had just changed her life…shaken the core of what she thought she knew about herself. One kiss from this man had opened a door she'd determined to keep closed—the door to future expectations. Oh yes, the damage was done. And Rebecca had absolutely no idea how to fix it.

Dinner that night was very quiet. Except for Jessie babbling in her high chair as she gnawed on a teething biscuit, that was.

Rebecca stared at her plate and pretended she found the sight of a fried pork chop thrilling. She didn't want to hurt Smoke's feelings, so she pushed the meat and the bone around her plate, wishing J.D.'s dog, Biscuit, was allowed under the table so she could slip her some food.

J.D., on the other hand, ate methodically. But he didn't say a word, either. Rebecca could feel Smoke peering at first one of them then the other. He tried to start a conversation.

"That cow done yet?"

J.D. responded with a sharp negative shake.

"Been going at it for a long time, ain't she, boy?"

This time J.D. gave an affirmative nod.

"Think she's gonna be all right? Should I call the Doc?"

That caught Rebecca's attention. "Do we have a sick cow?"

J.D. sent her a funny look. Before he could say anything, Smoke chuckled and declared, "No sicker than any woman is after she's been covered by a randy young stud, I reckon."

Rebecca jumped. The image of her and J.D. on the floor was burned on her brain and Smoke's comment brought it to life. She peeked at J.D. *What had he told Smoke?*

J.D. jerked to his feet. "Jeez, Smoke. What kind of talk is that?"

Perplexed, the older man shook his head. "I'm talking about that pregnant cow out there in the barn. Whaddaya think I'm talking about?"

Rebecca drew a sigh of relief. Smoke was talking about a rancher's hopeful conclusion to animal sex, not her own recent aborted sexual experience. She could relate to being covered by a randy young male. Although technically, she'd been the one to do the covering. Rebecca only hoped the cow had enjoyed it as much as she had—initially. She swallowed an almost hysterical giggle. Having something in common with a cow wasn't an everyday occurrence for her.

"Miss Chandler isn't used to hearing those kinds of matters discussed so freely at the dinner table."

"Since when are ya callin' her *miss?*" Smoke stroked his scraggly chin and narrowed his eyes to consider the tall man standing by the table, next to the same high chair that had once belonged to him. "You're being awfully formal to the woman who used your old raggedy underwear to polish the furniture today, aren't you, boy?"

To Rebecca's amazement, J.D. started to blush. Not everywhere at once, but selectively. First his neck, then his nose and finally the tips of his ears turned bright red. It was so cute—like a little boy caught in mischief. She hadn't seen this youthful side of him before. She wanted to squeeze him and tell him not to worry. Rebecca tried to take the focus off J.D. After all, she was the one responsible for his black mood.

"Do I understand you right, Smoke? Is there a cow in labor?" Interested, she looked from Smoke to J.D. "Can I help?" Since he was working so hard to keep her at arm's length, maybe this would be an opportunity to make J.D. understand why she couldn't get involved with him.

J.D. scowled back at her. "What do you know about labor?"

She smiled as she recognized the uncertainty J.D. was covering up with typical male bluster. "I don't know anything, but that's never stopped me before. May I visit her?"

"*Visit* the cow?" J.D. placed his palms flat against the table and leaned forward. "This isn't a tea party or some little play you see on your TV screen, city girl. This is life or death to a rancher. Cows and calves are a big part of the lifeblood of this ranch."

Rebecca placed her hand on his arm, needing to try to soften his anger toward her. "Then that's all the more reason for me to be there, in case you need a woman's touch." She felt his arm tremble under her fingers. At least he wasn't indifferent.

J.D. jerked as if she'd just pressed a red-hot branding iron against his skin. He pulled his arm away and ground his fists against his hips, stepping closer to the high chair. "If there's one thing I don't need, it's a woman's touch."

At that moment, with a delighted squeal, Jessie threw her biscuit down and grabbed for her uncle's sleeve. Startled, J.D. looked down at the baby, who now had a fistful of his shirt. His face softened as he stared at the grinning baby. He gently detached her grasp and placed his index finger on her nose, wiggling it back and forth. "Well, maybe you're an exception, short stuff."

Jessie immediately tried to reach for his hand and drew it into her mouth. "Oh, no you don't." J.D. withdrew his hand and hooked his thumb around his belt loop. He looked at Rebecca, who was once again charmed by his response to his niece. "What's with this kid? Doesn't she get enough to eat?"

"Babies are very tactile creatures at this age. Everything goes in their mouths for examination."

Jessie tried to reach for his hand again. "You'd better give her something more tasty than a hunk of western meat. It might corrupt her taste buds."

Flushing at his dig, Rebecca said, "I said I was sor—" She felt the dart of Smoke's sharp gaze and forced herself to say instead, "Why don't you help her eat? I'm sure she'd like that."

He stared at her, then at Jessie, who was now sucking happily on her own fingers. "I... have things I need to do in the barn."

"It won't take long, J.D."

"No. It's not a good idea."

"J.D.," Rebecca said gently, "one meal is not a commitment. To anyone." Let's start again, she thought, forget this afternoon ever happened. She shivered at the sudden hot flare of gold in his hazel eyes as they met hers. *If we can.*

"That depends on your point of view." J.D. started to

back up as his eyes dropped to her mouth. "Sometimes a taste is all you need to cause trouble."

Rebecca could feel the intensity of his gaze sear her lips. For a moment her mind went blank. Once again she felt Smoke's curious look slice between the two of them. She dragged her eyes away from J.D.

Smoke cleared his throat and stood up. Grabbing a few plates, he hustled over to the sink to scrape them.

"I'm going for a walk," J.D. announced.

Looking over his shoulder, Smoke said, "I thought you were going to the barn, boy?"

"Well, I'm going for a walk, then going to the barn."

"Why don't you go to the barn, then go for a walk. *Miss Chandler* and the baby would probably like to see the property at night." He turned around and leaned against the sink, an unlikely cupid, but an appealing one to Rebecca.

Not that she wanted someone to play cupid. After all, she'd kissed J.D. earlier because she wanted to take away his sadness, or his anger, or was it his hurt? As she peeked from Smoke to J.D., who was standing as still and rigid as a cactus in the face of Smoke's heavy-handed suggestion, she forced herself to respond honestly.

Face it, Rebecca. You kissed him because he's the sexiest man you've ever seen in your life. And there's no way in your day-to-day existence you'll ever run into someone like him again. Give yourself a break. Sometimes you just have to grab the moment or regret it forever. Your life is full of enough regrets.

"What a great idea." She flashed a look of gratitude toward Smoke, then glanced back to J.D. "We'd love to take a walk with you, J.D. Just let me feed Jessie, then clean her up. We can meet you outside the barn in about twenty minutes." Not giving J.D. a chance to deny her, Rebecca turned her back on him and started opening the baby food jars she had warming in a shallow bowl of hot water on the table. Rebecca started shoveling the food into

Jessie's mouth, afraid to take her time in case J.D. disappeared on her.

He tried.

Even over the sound of Smoke running water for dishes, she heard the door slamming behind J.D. as he went out into the night. Rebecca risked a peek over her shoulder at Smoke. She wasn't sure what to say, when Smoke took the matter out of her hands.

"I helped raise that boy after his daddy died, but I can't do much more for him. He's been solitary for quite a while." Turning the water off, he indicated the baby. "I want him to get to know that little one and see what the possibilities are in life again. I want him to hope an' dream. Like he used to before Rosalie left." He stared at Rebecca and suddenly Rebecca saw a caring old man who was worried sick about someone he loved. "Now, I don't know what you got in mind—if anything—but I don't want you to hurt him. He's been hurt enough."

Her mouth suddenly dry, Rebecca licked her lips. "I accidentally hurt him today, Smoke, but I don't want to hurt him anymore. I'm not sure what I want, but hurting him isn't part of it." She sighed. "He's so far from the type of man I know. I guess I'm curious. No it's more than that...I'm drawn to him because of it. But you don't have to worry about that. I'm so far from the type of woman he needs that it's laughable. I could never fit into his life. Anymore than he could fit into mine. We both know it." Automatically her fingers stroked her lips. "But maybe we could help each other somehow."

Smoke studied her for a moment. Then he leaned back against the sink with a relieved expression. "Well, you'd better get that little one cleaned up and get out there or that boy might walk himself right to California before you catch up with him."

Rebecca wasted no time following Smoke's instructions.

* * *

J.D. strode through the yard, across the grass and headed up the gravel drive to the outbuildings. Passing the horse corral, he gave a soft whistle and watched as his favorite horse, Whiskers, came up to the fence and hung his head over. With a soft whicker, Whiskers bumped his face against J.D.'s shoulder, then immediately lifted his head with a quick movement to knock J.D.'s hat off.

"Up to your old tricks, are you?" Laughing softly, J.D. reached over to pick up the hat. He slapped it against his thigh to get rid of any dust. Rubbing Whiskers' velvety nose, he grinned as the horse's eager lips nibbled at his shirt pocket. "Sorry, boy. I came out so fast, I forgot your carrots. I had other things on my mind." With a disgusted snort, Whiskers backed away.

Boy did he ever!

Ever since this afternoon, J.D.'s mind had been full of a brunette with the face of an angel and the body of the devil's key disciple. He'd managed to see her in two completely different moods today—and both had tempted him. He remembered her laugh—a light, lilting sound that could ride on the wind to make the bells jealous. When it had been accompanied by Jessie's hearty baby chortles, his heart had cramped with pain. His mother had had such laughter—the kind that made you ache to sit back and let it soothe the troubled spots in your soul. Even at fifteen, so had his sister, *damn her hide.* How long had it been since his house rang with a woman's merriment? Hearing those sounds in his own living room once again made him long for repetition…daily repetition. Which was ridiculous. He'd vowed not to get involved again—with anyone. He'd been tapped out, first by his fiancée, then by his sister dancing on his heart. He wouldn't let it happen again. But, God bless, he was tempted…tempted to all get-out by her laughter. Then driven positively insane with desire by her taste.

Her taste.

Unable to stand still, he started to walk again. He

couldn't figure how it had happened. One minute he'd been throwing a hissy fit over the woman rearranging his desk. And the next, he was flat on his back with the same woman rearranging his insides, turning them to mush. Shaking his head, he walked on past the barn door.

Damn all women, anyway!

He hesitated, then stepped through the doorway to peek inside at the pregnant cow now lying placidly in the straw in a nearby stall. "Everything all right, girl?" He didn't expect an answer. Nor was he yet alarmed. This was a first calving and sometimes they took awhile. All the same, he was positive he'd be sleeping in the barn tonight, keeping this cow company. He chuckled as he thought how earlier he'd been hoping to sleep with a different sort of female companion. The smile wiped off his face like a bad spill soaked up from a countertop. *God, that would have been a mistake.*

He knew she'd been as shaken by their contact as he'd been, which is why she'd tried to rationalize her behavior. He recognized her tactics. He'd tried the same himself whenever he was out of his depth. By reducing their shared desire to the appeal of "Western mystique and cowboy lore," Rebecca had tried to make it acceptable, if not understandable to herself. Well fine, J.D. thought. Intellectually he could understand that response, but emotionally was a different story. Emotionally he was torn up inside.

Ripped apart because she'd pretended to look at him as if he were an object—a generic cowboy. A man who didn't stick around to get involved because he never got off his horse long enough to stay in someone's life. Well, that wasn't it. That wasn't why he'd shut himself off to any future other than making the ranch work. No, J.D. shut himself off because he didn't want anyone to know the truth, any more than he wanted to face it. Fact was, he, the man following in his father's footsteps as a risk taker, was a fraud. J. D. McCoy was afraid. He was afraid of loving, afraid of being left, afraid of hoping. Now, with the arrival of Jessie and Rebecca—he was more than afraid. He was terrified. Terrified because he'd started to feel again. Started to question and wonder and dream…just a tiny bit.

With Rebecca, for the first time in a long time he remembered who he really was—J. D. McCoy, sole head of the family and proprietor of the Rio Rojo Ranch. He was all that was left of the legendary McCoys. J.D. also remembered his ultimate responsibility. He was going to make his mark on the world. But who was going to be around to notice? To carry on what he'd built?

Needing to move, he tore out of the barn, his long strides covering the ground until he reached the chicken coop at the far end of the yard. Slamming to a stop, he took a deep breath. The hens clucked softly as they rearranged themselves for the night. A slight breeze fluttered the leaves on the trees. Welcoming the air, J.D. pushed his hat to the back of his head, lifted his face and allowed the soft breeze to play over his cheeks, cooling the anxiety that had been building in him since he got his first real taste of Rebecca.

He hadn't been joking when he'd told her that sometimes one taste of a forbidden meal could lead to more trouble than a man wanted. Since this afternoon, he'd found himself imagining a future when his mouth could plunder hers, again and again and again…never tiring of it. Each day he'd discover more and more about the woman he'd held in his arms. How stupid could he get.

He took off his hat, slapped it against his thigh, then jammed it back on. *This is all my imagination. I've been without a woman for too long.*

Come to think of it, that was true. It had been quite a while. Somehow he'd lost the taste even for casual pleasure until Rebecca came along. And why Rebecca, he had no idea. The damn woman had *pain in the butt* written all over her. Look at the way she'd barged into his life, and immediately started redoing it. Without intending to do so, he was making tea, setting up baby beds, and appreciating a dust-free room for the first time in—how many months? *Next thing you know, I'll be bathing babies and cooking!*

Rebecca would laugh at that. He slammed his fist into the palm of his other hand. *Rebecca.* He couldn't get the damn woman out of his mind. Why, he had no idea. Granted she was a stunner, but he'd known good-looking women before with better bodies. A flare of tingling passion ran across his nerves as he remembered the feel of that body pressed against him. Hers had fit perfectly with his, every peak and valley seeming a part of the puzzle. Better bodies? More voluptuous bodies maybe, but not better.

He worked a bit harder to convince himself that Rebecca was only a temporary aberration. *The woman's not perfect. She's bossy and totally clueless about my type of life.* Yep, that right there should make him back away from her faster than a horse confronted with a rattlesnake. And that's what she was, he told himself, a serpent slithering up to him, using her wiles to twist him to her will.

A noise behind him made him turn, just in time to see Rebecca, with the baby in her arms, trip over an unseen root and almost go flying. Before J.D. could move though, she righted herself, stopping to check Jessie before she put one foot tentatively in front of the other to walk toward the barn. Unable to stop it, J.D. let a chuckle escape. *For a seductive serpent, she was pretty clumsy.* He supposed he'd better go get her before she and the baby fell into a pig trough or something. He refused to admit that the sight of her restirred all the longings he'd put into perspective a moment before. J.D. wondered what she intended to accomplish coming out here like this. Was she going to try to apologize again? Should he let her?

J.D. walked over to her, the darkness of the night scarcely affecting him. "Rebecca."

Near the corral, Rebecca started and whirled around. "J.D.? Is that you?"

"Nobody else."

"It's black as pitch out here. Where's the moon?"

"Same as it is back east, gone. Ready to start the month all over again."

"It's so dark outside. Last night I didn't realize it was quite this dark. Although I knew it was dark. Very dark. But I thought there'd be a light somewhere. Something to— I'm babbling aren't I? Like some…tenderfoot?"

"A little bit." He was surprised she'd admit it. His gaze sharpened as he took in the slight tremor near her lips. Was she nervous about the dark, or being alone with him? For some reason that perked him up a bit.

"Ahhh…gee…oohh." Jessie added her two cents' worth.

J.D. chuckled. "Jessie's babbling, too, if it makes you feel any better."

Smiling, Rebecca hiked the baby higher in her arms. "It would if she wasn't six months old." She squinted as she tried to peer at him through the darkness. "Where would you like to take us?"

J.D. thought about that for a moment, not sure if the answer was straight to town and the nearest airport, or tuck them both into bed. Jessie into hers and Rebecca into his. He settled for saying, "It's a bit too dark tonight to walk safely with the baby. Why don't I introduce you to my favorite old friend instead?"

"Oh, you have company." Rebecca looked around, obviously searching for a car. "I didn't hear anyone pull up, or honk for that matter."

"Well, he doesn't exactly have a horn." With that, he took Rebecca by the elbow and ushered her over to the corral. Even the soft touch of her arm stirred him. Once again he realized that for his own self-preservation he needed to put as much distance as possible between himself and this woman. When they reached the fence, J.D. made a soft clicking sound and the horse came running.

Rebecca backed up. "Oh, my God."

"Now, Reb, don't do that. You'll give him a complex."

"He's too damn big for me to give him a complex."

"Outside maybe, but inside this old boy is just a big bag of mush."

"Well, it's his outside I'm worried about."

J.D. reached for her. "Now stop that, and come over here. I want Jessie to meet Whiskers."

Putting one cautious foot in front of the other, Rebecca advanced, keeping a wary eye on the horse. "Why do you call him Whiskers? That's a funny name for a horse like this. There's no dignity in it."

"He's called Whiskers 'cause he has some white hairs just around his chin, like a goatee. But that wasn't a good name so Rosalie named him Whiskers." He remembered how happy she'd been the day Whiskers was born. Lord, how the memories had opened up today. But he didn't intend to get caught by them again.

Just then Jessie got his attention. With a charming gurgle, the baby leaned over from Rebecca's arms toward the horse. She spread her chubby arms wide and reached for Whiskers' head before Rebecca could react and pull her away.

"No leave them be, Rebecca. It's all right." J.D. laughed as the horse allowed the baby to stroke and touch his face, even going so far as stepping closer to inhale Jessie's scent.

Trying to hold on to the squirming baby, Rebecca said, "He's not going to eat her is he?"

"Not unless she tastes like a carrot." He stepped closer behind Rebecca to keep her from backing up. Stretching an arm over her shoulder he patted Whiskers and managed to detach the baby's fists from Whiskers' ear before she yanked. He knew from firsthand experience how much her yanks hurt! "Okay, that's enough, Jessie. Let go now."

Not at all happy with the interruption, the baby turned

her head sharply and glared at J.D. Her chin jutted forward and so did her bottom lip as she stared at him.

Suddenly he recognized himself in that look. It was the same one he gave the world when it told him he couldn't do something and he dared it to take its best shot. That's when it hit him…slamming into his gut so sharply that his hand froze with Jessie's fist trapped inside his. *This child is a McCoy, too. She has as much right to be here as I do.*

Rebecca stirred against his body as his arm dropped like a fallen tree limb to rest on her shoulder. "J.D.? Are you all right?"

It took a moment before he could respond. "Yeah. Fine. Just thinking."

"Thinking what?"

Thinking what? His thoughts skittered this way and that as he tried to focus on what this could mean.

"J.D. What's the—?" The alarm in her voice finally penetrated.

"Uh…yeah…thinking, uh…" He stepped forward and pulled the baby away from the horse, who backed up in relief. J.D. watched his favorite horse suddenly turn tail and prance away. Damn, he wished he could join him.

"J.D.?"

"I'm just thinking, I'm going to teach you to ride."

"You're what?" Rebecca's voice rose so high it squeaked.

Still shaken by his realization, he moved away, then turned around and leaned his arms against the railing. He stared from her to the baby, then back again. "Yeah. It's a good idea. I'll get you up on a horse then maybe take Jessie up on one, too, and we'll all take a ride."

Rebecca backed away. "I—don't—think—so! There's no way I'm riding something that big. And this baby is definitely not getting up on one, either. So, don't mention it again."

"As to that, Reb, this baby has Western blood running

through her veins. Horses and cattle are as much a part of her as the air and earth. If she's going to spend some time here, she's got to find out where she comes from, and what she's made of." By God, it was time he started focusing on the same thing. How could he let this woman throw him a curve like she had? After all, he was J. D. McCoy and this ranch was his home. It was time to stop running and face it. Who knew what he'd discover about himself in the process?

"J.D., that's ridiculous. She's only a baby, for heaven's sake."

"You're never too young to learn who you are, or where you belong. Or too old, either." He stared down at her, challenging the spirit he knew she used to face up to her everyday world. "If she's going to stay—and I don't know if I see any way around it at the moment—she needs to make friends with a horse. So do you. Since it seems you'll be here for a time yourself…like it or not."

"I do like it. At least, I think I do." Confused, she glanced around, peering through the dark at the landscape. "I just don't understand it. Not like you do."

"Well now, Rebecca, that's what's so good about being such a dull, boring man. I don't have to look for meaning." Damn, he'd sworn he'd keep his hurt feelings over her comments buried, and here they rushed right out and tripped him when he wasn't looking.

"Oh, J.D. None of that came out right this afternoon. I was embarrassed so I stupidly tried to reduce my feelings to black and white instead of—"

"I know." J.D. held up his hand. "It's not important anymore, though. What's important is this little one here. I don't see as I have any choice but to help her experience her heritage." Trying to convince himself that his acceptance of Jessie was logical, not emotional, J.D. dropped a quick, casual kiss on the baby's head. Before he could back away, Jessie leaned toward him and pressed another wet, sloppy baby smooch on his cheek.

Chuckling, he drew back and looked at the little girl. "What did I tell you about kissing strange men?"

Rebecca laughed. "It kills me how affectionate she is. Rosalie must have given her lots of kisses, 'cause when I give her a kiss, she puckers up and gives me one back."

J.D. stared at the grinning baby as he felt one more hunk of the ice around his heart start to crack.

7

Rebecca's eyes flew open. Confused, she looked around her bedroom. Nothing out of the ordinary, she thought. Twisting, she glanced at the travel clock on the desk behind her and groaned. Automatically she reached her hand down to pat Jessie, then remembered she was now sleeping in Rosalie's old room. She listened for a telltale sound from the baby monitor she'd purchased before she left Boston. No sound from the baby, but...there it was again.

Rebecca sat up and cocked her head, listening intently. It had been a scraping noise. She threw back the sheet and rose to her knees to look out the window. Why, she had no idea, as it was still as black as a liar's heart outside. She couldn't see a darn thing but weird, black outlines. Then a small sliver of light sliced across the bare ground in front of the barn.

J.D.

As she watched, he slipped inside the large wooden structure and pulled the door shut after him. Darkness reigned once again.

"It must be the cow." Rebecca couldn't think of anything else that would take him out into the barn in the middle of the night. She nibbled a finger then decided, "Might as well see for myself!" See for herself what being part of a ranch was all about. After all, he might need some help.

Rebecca scrambled from the bed, immediately bumped into the desk chair, swore and hopped around for a moment, holding her big toe. Rather than risk rousing the baby by her further blunderings, she reached for the light. She rummaged through her suitcase.

"What does one wear to a cow birthing?"

Then she groaned. Good thing J.D. hadn't heard that inane comment. Hesitating, she stared at the bright jumble of clothing and realized she had not packed as appropriately as she might have for this Texas trip. Of course she hadn't expected to stay put on a ranch, but still! Finally, she extracted a pair of tailored beige chinos and a short-sleeved red camp blouse and threw them on. After slipping her feet into brown leather moccasins, and slipping the remote receiver for the baby monitor in her pocket, she opened her door a few inches and squeezed though the narrow opening into the hallway. Rebecca tiptoed past Jessie's room, holding her breath in case the baby accidentally heard her and woke up. Then she remembered, not only was Smoke sleeping downstairs but this was the child who slept through most everything—but new teeth—and she didn't worry quite as much. As a matter of fact, Jessie had been remarkably quiet about her teething process all evening. Maybe the tooth had cut through the gum. Surely that would make the pain easier to bear? Rebecca grimaced, wishing she knew more about babies!

Rebecca reached the stairs and tiptoed down, freezing when one of the old treads cracked. The house stayed still around her, the silence friendly somehow, unlike the quiet houses in which she'd grown up. There the stillness had had a frozen quality. But not here. Here, there remained the certainty of the love that had surrounded the people who lived under this roof.

Until Rosalie had run away and left confusion and pain in her wake.

With a deep sigh, Rebecca ran her hand along the railing.

The wood was so smooth. Smooth from the loving grip of generations of hands—one family, not the variety of ancestors Rebecca had temporarily been part of. What was that like, she wondered. The ability to look in a mirror and know your own great-grandmother had done so, many times before you. A thrill ran up Rebecca's spine. This house spoke of continuity and belonging. How lucky J.D. was. He didn't realize it, had lost sight of it for the moment, but it was there.

Anxious to see J.D. and the beginning moments of a new family, Rebecca hurried down the stairs and out the door to pick her way across the yard, not stopping until she reached the barn. A low vibration of sound reached her ears through the old wooden door. She tilted her head to listen. *Humming. Someone is humming.* Enchanted, she pulled on the handle and stepped inside the barn into J.D.'s world.

J.D. was kneeling in the cow's stall with his back toward the door. He was crooning a lullaby to the laboring mother, now lying on the straw. "Close the door, Smoke."

Hastily Rebecca did so, saying, "It's not Smoke. It's me."

J.D. threw her a look over his shoulder. "Rebecca? What are you doing here? Do you know what time it is?"

"Uh-huh." Rebecca nodded. "About two o'clock."

"You should be sound asleep."

"Something woke me up."

J.D. looked guilty. "That must have been me. The drawer in my desk sticks and I have to yank it good to open it sometimes."

"Is there something you needed in the house? Should I go back and—"

He held up a syringe and an empty medication bottle. "No, I got it."

"You had to give the cow a shot?"

"She's about at the end of her rope. I wanted to help

her with her contractions. If this doesn't work, I'll have to call the vet.''

Rebecca walked over to the stall and leaned against the open door. ''I should have thought you'd call him before this.''

''Nah. You can't call a vet for every little thing. Ranchers learn to do a lot of doctoring on their own. You save the vet for when you've got an emergency you can't handle. Vets are expensive, you know.'' He smoothed a gentle hand over the cow's side.

Rebecca didn't, but she nodded as if she did.

J.D. caught her at it. ''That's right. I forgot. You were the kid without any pets, weren't you?''

Stung, Rebecca replied, ''You make it sound as if it's a capital offense.''

''Might as well be, in my opinion. What were your parents thinking of?''

''It depends which set of parents you're talking about.''

''Huh?''

''Well there was husband-father-type number one who didn't care for children, especially not little children. But Mother divorced him because his business went down the tubes faster than their marriage. Then there was husband-father number two, who felt children should be seen, but only at the appropriate moments, and never heard—he and Mother had 'irreconcilable differences.' After him was husband number three, who had political ambitions, but no fatherly ambitions. Then—''

''God, Reb. How many times did your mother marry?''

''Including the last?'' As J.D. nodded, she bit her lip, then whispered, ''Six.'' By now admitting her mother's proclivity for weddings was almost old hat, but Rebecca still found it painful. ''The sixth time was the charm, though. At least, it has been so far. Mother is into year eight of this marriage.'' Even as she tried to pretend it didn't bother her, she was certain he knew she was lying when he threw her a look over his shoulder that penetrated into the dark, pain-filled cavities she hid deep inside.

Finally he said, "Sometimes people have to keep looking until they find what's really right for them. It's hard to understand from the outside, or even when you're in the middle of it, but everybody goes about things differently, I reckon. Now, maybe your mama just couldn't find what she was meant for the first time."

Rebecca walked closer to the stall and leaned on the rails. "I think that's a very generous assessment of my mother's actions, J.D." Her lips twisted as if she'd just tasted a sour fruit. "Especially when you consider her many promises to love—"

"Maybe what she was really looking for was security, not love. To some people security comes first and when it finally happens, the love builds day by day, afterward. So for your mama, the sixth time might have really been the charm."

Rebecca was silent as she chewed over his response. She met his gaze, his eyes so warm and compelling, so understanding, so—unexpected. She hadn't expected this response from a man like him. Especially when she considered his family history—one family, one ranch, one united purpose. However, as much as she appreciated what J.D. was trying to say, she couldn't quite equate such selfless behavior with her mother. "To my mother, security equaled money and position. That's what matters to her."

"Hell, Rebecca, it matters to a lot of people. That doesn't make her the Wicked Snow Queen or something does it?"

Surprised, Rebecca giggled. "Maybe not. Close though, because she sure didn't consider the effect a new parent every week would have on me."

"Well, as to that," J.D. drawled, "it's hard to understand why people do what they do unless you've walked in a body's boots." He lifted an eyebrow and considered her for a moment. "Maybe your mother thought doing what was best for her would ultimately be what was the best for you.''

"Sort of like you and Rosalie, you mean?'' She'd startled him. She could tell by the painful stretch of his lips—a smile that hurt, she thought. Would they be able to work through the pain if Rosalie came back? For J.D.'s sake she hoped so. But if Rosalie didn't come back, would J.D. really be able to accept Jessie? To accept the tangible proof of how far Rosalie's rebellion had taken her? It was something she hadn't considered before.

Before J.D. could respond to her, the cow let out a low bellow and seemed to gather all of her energies, ready to push. Hurriedly, J.D. reached to his side and plunged his hands into a bucket of water. He lathered his hands with the big bar of soap, then he stripped off his shirt and moved into position behind the cow. "Okay, girl. What do you say we introduce this young one to everyone."

Fascinated, Rebecca stepped inside the stall. She watched intently as J.D. positioned himself to bring a new life into the world. "Easy now, sweetheart. Any minute and you'll be a new mama.'' His voice was a lullaby. With the realization of how gentle this tough Texan could be, Rebecca took another step toward falling in love. No, not love, she corrected herself, admiration.

"Son of a bit—'' He bit off his comment, groaned and then his deep tan paled a shade as the cow strained against his arm.

Rebecca sidled around the edge of the cow's pen. "My God, J.D., doesn't that hurt?''

Exhaling, J.D. said, "I've had a better time, Reb.''

"No, really?'' Smiling, Rebecca bent over, trying to snatch a closer look from her location, which was still removed from the main event. "I don't see anything yet. Where's the baby?''

J.D. ignored her question and let out a long, fluid string of some of the best expletives Rebecca had ever heard. And with the type of clientele she generally worked with, she'd heard quite a few. After a moment, Rebecca whistled. "Very impressive."

J.D. caught himself and sent her an apologetic look. "Sorry, about that. But I think I've got twins."

"Twins. That's wonderful!"

"No. That's the problem. One of them's stuck and my hand's too big to slip past the bottleneck and untangle them. I'll have to call the vet and hope he can get here in time."

"And if he doesn't?"

"I'll probably lose the cow and the calves."

Rebecca covered her mouth, trying to keep the horror inside. She couldn't. "They'll die, you mean?"

J.D. backed his arm out and sat up, reaching for a towel. "Could be." His earlier excitement had evaporated. He set his jaw in a look Rebecca was beginning to recognize. The one that clearly said he was ready to deal with whatever fate might have in store.

Rebecca rushed forward and dropped to her knees. She stroked the heaving side of the laboring cow. "There, now. It's going to be okay."

"It is, huh? How do you figure that?"

She stared at her manicured hand as it rested on the cow's hide, the immaculate polish contrasting sharply with her current surroundings. She'd never been this close to an animal like this in her life. Rebecca could feel the sharp bristles of the cow's hide under her fingers and hear the quick pants as the cow struggled to give birth. The sharp tangy scent of the animal combined with the sweet smell of the fresh hay on which she lay. Then the cow lifted her head and looked at Rebecca. Her large brown eyes looked worried. Worried as only a mother's could. The cow also looked beaten, conquered, as if she knew her hopes and dreams weren't taking their natural course and she couldn't figure out why. Rebecca couldn't ignore that look. It was looks like that from children and adults at the end of their ropes that had led her into social services in the beginning. And the reason she'd started burning out when she found she couldn't put the job in it's proper perspective and forget them. Those looks haunted her day and night...expressions of hopelessness, of despair... *No, by God. Not if I can help it!*

"Hold on, girl." Rocking back on her heels, she twisted and pierced J.D. with a look. She help up her hand. "My hands are smaller than yours. What do I have to do?"

J.D. obviously couldn't believe his ears as he stared at her, his gaze skimming over her immaculate clothing. He shook his head. "Beg pardon?"

Scrambling to her to her feet, Rebecca moved around to the bucket of water and plunged her hands inside, grimacing at the cold. She grabbed hold of the bar of soap and lathered up. Giving him an impatient look over her shoulder, she repeated, "J.D., wake up. What do you want me to do?"

J.D. picked up an old feed sack and wiped his hand and arm off before replying. "Are you telling me that you want to help with this cow, Rebecca?"

"What—" She regained her calm and nailed him with a brief smile. "J.D., did your brain go on vacation when I wasn't looking? Of course, I do! I can't stand by and let this cow die. Not when I might be able to help."

"You've never even taken care of a pet, and now you're telling me that you're all primed up to help this cow birth a calf?"

She couldn't blame the man for thinking she'd lost her mind. Part of her wondered if maybe she had.

J.D. snorted like a restless horse. "Rebecca, you're nuts. I'm calling the vet."

"You said yourself, the vet won't make it in time."

J.D. let his gaze wander over her attire, giving her one

last way to change her mind. "You're not exactly dressed for—"

"That doesn't matter."

J.D. stared at her, wondering if he was actually sound asleep and this was some type of offbeat nightmare. As she tapped her foot, waiting for him to make up his mind, her impatient look almost made him chuckle. However, J.D. swallowed it and his incredulity. He took a moment more and assessed the woman opposite him. From her earnest face to the tense set of her shoulders, and the alert position of her body she looked committed to action. She lifted her chin, set her lips and met his gaze head-on. The fierce resolve in her eyes overcame all of his reservations.

Lord, she reminds me of my mother when she got on her high horse.

Shaken by the thought, he wiped a bead of sweat from his brow with his forearm. *Okay, McCoy, get a grip here.* This might be his only shot to save this cow, and he couldn't afford to take the loss. He nodded. "What the hell. Okay, Reb, let's get you in position."

"Right."

J.D. helped Rebecca get behind the mother-to-be and settled down next to her to coach. He glanced back at the cow, who was now apathetically staring at the opposite wall. "She seems to have stopped pushing." That worried him. He hated to see an animal give up like that.

"Don't worry, J.D. I can do this. We Boston women are tough!"

Chuckling, J.D. rubbed her shoulder, trying to convey all of his faith in her into that one gesture. "I'm beginning to believe it."

Rebecca dug her toes into the straw and stretched forward. After a few moments, she turned an eager face toward him. "I can feel a leg, and something that feels like a hoof."

J.D. grinned at her excitement. "That's the problem.

There are a bunch of little legs in the way. Now all you have to figure out is, who belongs to what.''

Rebecca flashed him a grin. "Piece of cake."

Smiling back, he watched Rebecca settle in and concentrate on the job before glancing back to check again on the lethargic mother.

"Oh, J.D.... I think I've found the problem. One's blocking the way. They're jammed up in here like the rush-hour traffic into the Boston Tunnel."

"Then it's time to push that calf back and turn this red light to green." Excited now, he lay down behind her and helped support Rebecca as she pushed with all her might.

After a moment, Rebecca said, "I think the calf is moving backward, J.D."

Lifting his head, J.D. looked over the animal's rump. The cow had suddenly raised her head and shoulders and taken on a much more businesslike demeanor. "Okay. I think you did it, Reb. Back off. Let's see if mom and Mother Nature can do the rest."

Once Rebecca had rinsed her hands in the water once more and dried off, J.D. yanked her out of the way. Taking her with him, he scooted backward, until he leaned his spine against the stall boards. He wrapped his arms around Rebecca, who sat within his cocked legs, with her back against his chest and her firm little bottom snuggled smack against the crotch of his jeans. He was vaguely aware of the cow in front of him as his attention went instead to the woman nestled in his arms. She felt so right there. Just like she belonged. Like she'd come home. His arms tightened under her chest as he pulled her closer. He sighed and let his cheek fall against her fragrant hair. He inhaled... gardenias, he thought. He pressed his lips against her hair and felt her shiver.

Together, they sat and quietly watched the miracle of birth.

It never failed to delight J.D., no matter how many times

he saw it. He was happy Rebecca was there to share it with him. Neither of them moved or said a word until two new-born calves were deposited on the straw not far from their feet, but he knew how moved Rebecca was by the deep intake of air she'd taken after the last birth. He held her tighter as the calves' mother, with a deep, satisfied, chuckling sound, turned around to lick her babies and nuzzle them into movement. One of them didn't immediately respond.

J.D. started to reach around Rebecca. "I was afraid of this. I don't think one of them made it."

Placing her hand on his arm, Rebecca stopped him. "No, wait. It's okay. Look."

She was right. As J.D. watched, the second calf started to revive under his mother's rough tongue. Meanwhile, the first one tried to stagger to its feet.

Delighted, Rebecca laughed and peered at him over her shoulder. "We did it. We did it, J.D."

J.D. caught her chin in his hand and brought her face closer to his. "No, Reb, darlin'…you did it. Without you, there wouldn't be one of them left, much less three." He grinned as his gaze roamed over her dirt-smudged face. "If your society mother could only see you now, Ms. Chandler."

Rebecca grinned back. "She'd probably have a stroke."

"What she ought to do is stand up and cheer for her daughter. You've never been more beautiful." And it was true. To him, this woman was the most beautiful thing he'd ever seen.

"J.D.…." Rebecca's breath seemed to catch. Then it straightened out enough for her to say, "Are you serious? I've got bits of hay in my hair and I'm covered with—"

"I'm not talking about what you look like. I'm talking about who you are."

"Who I am?" Her eyes widened. The tip of her tongue peeped out to wet her lips. "Who am I?"

"A woman my mother would have been proud of." Unable to hold off any longer, he tasted her lips. Slowly he sank into them, relaxed and settled down to familiarity. True, he'd only tasted her once before, but he knew this woman. He remembered her with every fiber of his being. He extended his tongue, allowing himself the time to trace the edge of her lips before sliding inside her mouth. This, too, felt like home. As if he'd been here many times before and had only to take a brief moment to refamiliarize himself with her sweetness. Patiently he encouraged her to open farther, allowing him fuller access. His tongue touched hers, circling then slipping inside to reach deep into the recesses of her mouth. There all patience ended as she abruptly came to life in his arms...as her tongue moved forward to tangle with his, then start a probe of her own.

I can't get enough of her.

He tried to pull her closer, tucking her into his body and wrapping his legs around her until he couldn't tell where she ended and he began. Until he felt himself reeling off into the space...into the unknown, with emotions he'd never dreamed of before.

Damn he wanted her. He'd never wanted a woman this badly in his life. It shocked him to realize he didn't only want her body, he wanted her mind as well. He hadn't bargained for that. It scared the hell out of him, as a matter of fact. As the realization hit him, he fell back to earth with a thud. Painfully, he started the journey back to reality. Step by step he withdrew, first his tongue left hers, then his lips, then his hand dropped to his knee and finally he moved his legs, stretching one long leg until it paralleled hers instead of acting as a cocoon for her body. His eyes met hers and he almost melted at the churning passion...and the waves of confusion he saw in her stormy blue eyes. He jerked as if an electric current had just touched water. Why had he stopped? He must have been nuts. *I want her.* For a moment, he was ready to forget any reservations he might have

about making love to her. *Surely that would be enough.*
But would it be? How could he cope if it became more,
for either of them? More than that, how could he let her
go when the time came?

J.D. hesitated, unsure what to do next. Then from the
corner of his eye he saw the two small calves making their
way to their mother for their first meal.

Relief flooded over him. Was this what his unbelievable
response to her really meant? Was it gratitude for her actions that made her feel so right in his arms? Because he
knew he wasn't right for her. J.D. knew it as surely as his
mother was standing over his shoulder telling him so. Regardless of what he'd imagined for a moment, this was a
woman who would never be content on a small ranch in
the middle of nowhere. Thank God he hadn't opened his
mouth and said something he'd have trouble taking back.
There'd been enough impulsive words in his life. And
enough consequences based on them.

Instead he indicated the sight to their right. "Look at
that, Rebecca. Thanks to you, that's a nice little family."

He pretended not to notice that she had to visibly pull
her emotions back together to feign interest. Just as he tried
not to be hurt when she shrank away from him, moving a
bit to the side to stop any more contact with his body—
accidental or otherwise.

"A family," she whispered. "I came to Texas to create
a family."

"Well, you did. You've just given the Rio Rojo Ranch
a brand-new one." J.D. knew he was being overly hearty
and sounded false, but he wasn't sure what to do now. He
was so afraid that if he allowed a hint of his true feelings
to peek through, that he'd lose control and lower her back
into the straw and show her exactly how families started.
The fact that he suddenly wanted to start that family more
than anything in the world was almost as alarming as the
fact that this was the woman he wanted to start it with. His

heart ached as he watched Rebecca give a brief smile that was gone in an instant.

"Happy though I am about the outcome, J.D., this wasn't the family I had in mind."

J.D. studied her quietly for a moment. "Thank you, Rebecca." *Thank you for coming into my life at a time when I needed you to show me what I was missing.*

Surprised, she turned to look him full in the face. "For this, you mean?" She waved a hand in the direction of the mother and twins.

"Not just that. For everything you've done so far. I know I haven't made it too obvious, but I appreciate everything you've done for the McCoys. I really do."

He watched the color sweep over her face, tinting her high cheekbones a delicate pink before creeping around to accent her eyes. J.D. cleared his throat. "I don't know how I'll ever repay you." Although, now that he'd started to feel again, he thought it might be a mixed blessing.

"Oh, I think you've done enough. Any more repayment and I might not survive it." As the words spilled out, her hand flew toward her mouth where her lips trembled for an instant before she recovered her control and forced her arm down to her side.

"Rebecca, I wish…" He didn't know what else to say, so he allowed the thought to linger in the air like a night whisper. As he sought to put his feelings into words, Rebecca used the small reprieve to pull herself together.

With an attempt at cockiness, she shrugged. "Besides, it's all in a day's work. Anyone would have done the same."

J.D. chuckled. "Somehow I doubt that."

"All right. How about…any one of your strong and mighty Texas women would have done the same?"

"Somehow I doubt that, too."

She stood up, now seeming eager to leave him. "I have to go inside and take a shower. And check on the baby."

J.D. stopped her as she got on the other side of the stall door. ''Rebecca.''

She halted but didn't turn. ''What?''

''I didn't kiss you because I was grateful for what you did tonight.''

Her shoulders tensed. ''Then why did you kiss me, J.D.?''

He was silent for a moment, knowing he should have let her go. That would have been better for both of them. As he struggled to find the words to explain, she glanced back at him over her shoulder. When he met her eyes, he blurted the truth. ''Because I couldn't help myself. And I'm really afraid I'm going to be in the same boat any time I'm around you.''

To his surprise, Rebecca whirled around, looking as confused as he felt. ''That makes two of us.''

Struck by her assertive honesty, he challenged her back. ''What are we going to do about it?''

''Damned if I know.'' With that Rebecca spun on her heel, strode toward the barn door and slammed her way through it. When the echo died, the only sounds left were the deep, contented sounds of the new mother and the sucking of her two newborn calves. J.D. looked around the old wooden barn that had been here before he'd been born…where he had played as a child and worked as a man. It was all he'd ever known. All he thought he'd ever want.

For the first time, he wondered what it would be like to live in a city. To live near Rebecca.

8

———➤ ◄———

Rebecca crept into her bedroom and undressed in the dark. She didn't want to turn on a lamp and have to face her emotions in the light. Emotions which were still too raw to glimpse, much less touch. In the dark she could lick her wounds, as she tried to recover from the thrill of his passion and the pain of his rejection.

Her fingers trembled as she slipped the buttons of the blouse through the buttonholes. She tore off her top, then unsteadily struggled out of her pants and shoes. Rebecca pitched all of the grimy garments into the corner of the room. She knew, clean or not, she would never wear them again. She'd never be able to look at the blouse without remembering the way her breasts had pressed against his chest. Or look at the pants and not see his long legs tangled with hers. Every time she looked at those clothes she would think of kissing J.D. She would fantasize about making love to J.D. She would hunger for J.D. And that was the truth of it. The man made her ravenous for things she hadn't even known she wanted. Rebecca gulped down a sob and reached for her robe.

Leaving her room for a well-deserved shower, Rebecca recalled her duty long enough to stop outside Jessie's door and listen for any sounds of restlessness. Nothing. The baby was content. Rebecca only wished she was. She longed for the moral certainty with which she had come to Texas, for the status quo J. D. McCoy had disrupted with his lips, with his hands, with his humor and most of all with his need for her—all the more compelling because of how hard he was fighting it. Almost as hard as she was.

She dashed away a tear. *Damn the man for inspiring such feelings.*

Rebecca jerked back the old shower curtain and stepped inside the tub. Turning on the shower, she stood under the spray, letting the warm needles of water play over her skin. She felt as if she'd left a piece of herself back in the barn with J.D.

She lathered soap onto her skin, stroking the sponge over her shoulders, then down her breasts—remembering his touch. The man got under her skin like no one she'd ever known. It was all the more amazing when she considered how little time she'd actually known him. But it didn't feel like that. She had felt a depth of connection that might have been part of her history. If she'd had a history, that was. If she'd been anything other than the practical, pragmatic, realist she considered herself to be, she might have considered this fate. It would have been her destiny to travel here and meet J.D. It might have been her destiny to act completely out of character and impulsively bring a baby into the sphere of J.D.'s influence.

Rebecca clutched the sponge until the soap dripped onto the tub bottom and dissolved into nothingness. She had a friend who read tarot cards. For the first time she wondered if she should give her a call, because she honestly didn't know what to do next. She'd been perfectly truthful with J.D. She was very afraid that she couldn't keep her hands off him, anymore than he could keep his off her. A secret smile peeped out as Rebecca thought of how appealing she found that thought. How she'd like to feel his hands everywhere…his strong fingers pressing and stroking, bringing her to life. As no one else had before. Rebecca had a horrible suspicion that no one else would ever do it as successfully as he did ever again. She was afraid of what that might mean.

Her head now aching, Rebecca tried to focus on the only real option she felt she had. She'd have to put J. D. McCoy behind her and get on with her future. She'd have to put this entire night behind her...well, most of this night. She'd never forget her role in bringing a new life into the world. She'd carry the joy and satisfaction of that experience with her, no matter what else happened. At least that was something...something lasting, Rebecca thought. Something much more positive than her agony over J. D. McCoy's reluctance to connect with a woman.

With a sigh, she massaged her temples. Trying to find her professional self in the emotional woman this night had revealed, Rebecca forced herself to concentrate. Questions about her destiny were not the issue; she still had a job to do here in Texas. Then, and only then, could she make any decisions about her personal life. That decided, she turned off the tap, pulled back the curtain and reached for the towel. After drying off and belting her terry cloth robe, Rebecca opened the door and ran right into the subject of her most heated thoughts.

"Oh, my G—!"

J.D. grabbed her arm to steady her, clamping a hand over her mouth to muffle her scream. "Shhh, you'll wake the baby."

Rebecca yanked his hand down. "Please. Take your hands off me."

Stunned, J.D. dropped his arms to his side and stepped back. "You didn't seem to mind my hands on you earlier."

"That was then. This is now." She bit her lip as the words hung in the air.

He hesitated, then firmed his shoulders and said softly, "Rebecca, I know I didn't handle things right before. I'd like to—"

She rubbed her forehead. "Look J.D., I really can't take

much more tonight. I'd prefer we leave it as we did.'' If they didn't, she might say all kinds of words she wasn't even ready to think about, much less say.

His gaze wandered down to the plunging neckline of her robe. ''How did we leave it?''

Because she could feel her skin heating under his look and her breathing accelerating to match his, she clutched the neck of her robe in a tight fist to remove the temptation—from both of them. ''We left it alone, remember?''

A slight smile teased his lips. ''I remember letting you leave alone. Something I regret very deeply at the moment.''

Rebecca blinked hard to stop it, but an uncontrollable tear slipped over her lashes and ran down her cheek. *Only this man could be so absurd, and so endearing at the same time.*

''Oh, God.'' His finger touched her cheek and wiped away the tear. Amazed and appalled, he stared at the moisture on his fingertip. ''You're crying. I've made you cry.''

The big idiot! Of course he made her cry. What did he think—she was made of ice? ''It's not because of you. I have a headache.''

''Oh.'' He still stared at his finger, before his turbulent gaze lifted to meet hers. ''Can I do something for you? Help you some—''

''No.''

He stepped forward like an eager-to-please puppy. ''I can give you a neck massage. I give great massages.''

Rebecca just bet he did. But the thought of having his hands on her again without finishing the job was more than she could stand. She wanted him to touch her so much that she took two steps sideways to force herself to move down the hallway. ''No. I have to go to bed. So I can sleep off the pain.''

''I understand.''

No. No he didn't. He didn't understand at all. The big

lug just stood there and looked compassionate and sexier than any man had a right to. He didn't understand that she was tempted to throw him onto the carpet and ravage him. Damn, she didn't understand it, either! She just knew it was so, and getting stronger everytime she saw him. Without another word she whirled around and raced for her room, with his voice following her softly down the hall.

"Sweet dreams, Rebecca."

Fat chance!

Rebecca threw herself on the bed and yanked the sheet up to her ears, determined to forget the man. Unfortunately, it was easier said than done. He danced in and out of her dreams. However, at some point she must have fallen into a fitful sleep because the next thing she knew, the sun was slanting across her eyelids trying to wake her as insistently as a dedicated rooster. She groaned and rubbed her eyes. Her headache was gone, but she still felt groggy. Rebecca looked around J.D.'s old room. As her mind crept into some type of consciousness, her surroundings made her remember the reason she'd initially come here...something she'd almost forgotten the night before. She was here to bring a baby back to her family and her home. Recalled to her purpose, she glanced at the clock.

Ten-thirty! It can't be that late!

Jessie should have awakened for breakfast long before this. She never slept this late. Had something happened to her?

Rebecca leaped out of bed and raced to the next room. She slowed down as she crept up to the door. Reaching for the handle, she turned the knob and cautiously slid inside. Rosalie's room was much as she'd first seen it, but was now a bit more welcoming. Rebecca had taken care of that yesterday when J.D. had set up the baby bed, so that wasn't a surprise. What was a surprise was the empty crib. The scenarios of every suspense novel she'd ever read raced through her head. Finally she plucked the first theory she could think of...the only one that initially made sense to her emotionally exhausted mind.

Oh, my God, someone has kidnapped the baby!

This absurdity was swiftly followed by other more realistic ones. *Or else J.D. sent for someone to take her away. Or Rosalie has come home.*

Rebecca whirled around and was about to race for the stairs when she realized she was still wearing her robe. Swearing, she ran to her room, threw on some clothes, then hit the hallway like a thoroughbred. She clattered down the steps and promptly skidded on the rug at the bottom. Instinctively she grabbed for the newel post to stop her fall. Barely managing to keep herself upright, she galloped down the hall and burst into the kitchen.

"Smoke, where..." she yelled at the top of her lungs. Then she skidded to a stop as she took in the scene before her.

There was no Rosalie, but Jessie was there. She was sitting in her high chair covered with something that looked like baby cereal, while J.D. sat in front of her covered with a fair amount of the same substance. Both of them sent her an astonished look at her entrance. However, Jessie went one step further. She opened the little mouth stuffed with cereal and started to wail. Naturally gravity took its course and the sticky goo poured right out and down the front of her. The part that didn't spit toward J.D. first, that was.

"Ah, Reb, look what you did. I just managed to stuff a whole spoonful of this gunk into her. Now it's coming right back out."

For a moment Rebecca felt like Alice in Wonderland at the Mad Hatter's tea party. The more she stared, the more Jessie yelled. Her little arms started flailing around and landed in the cereal bowl that J.D. had unwisely placed on the tray in front of her. She sent it flying. Horrified, Rebecca watched as the bowl flew up and headed straight for

J.D.'s lap. Futilely she tried to move fast enough to catch it. No such luck.

J.D. must have seen it coming and attempted to avoid the same thing as he tried to scoot his chair backward to avoid the flying glop. But he overbalanced, and the chair fell over backward instead—and J.D. with it.

What goes up, must come down, Rebecca figured. And it did. Right on J.D.'s chest. After spilling the rest of its contents, the plastic bowl bounced off J.D. and landed on the floor with a sharp ping. Then, there was silence. Even Jessie had stopped crying as she leaned over her high chair to look at the large man sprawled at her feet.

This absolute stillness must be what occurs after a nuclear destruction, Rebecca thought as she looked away from J.D. around the room. Anyway, the kitchen did look like a bomb had gone off in it, with dishes and cereal and splashes of milk everywhere.

The silence was broken by the sound of a baby's laugh. A deep, hearty chuckle that made the corners of Rebecca's mouth twitch. Jessie was hanging over the side of her high chair, staring at her uncle and laughing like a comedian who'd just told the world's best joke.

It was a touchy thing for a moment as J.D. stared up at the amused baby. But he was no more immune to her sudden humorous charm than Rebecca was. To Rebecca's relief, he grinned back at Jessie. Then he turned his head to look at Rebecca.

"Thank God I didn't open the peaches, too."

Rebecca lost it! She started laughing so hard that she had to hang on to the doorjamb to keep herself upright. When J.D. pulled himself to a sitting position, gingerly plucking his soaked shirt away from his body, she laughed even harder.

"Oh...J.D....you should see yourself."

"I don't need to see myself. I've got a good imagination."

Walking forward, Rebecca extended her hand to take the messy bowl. "I don't think it's this good. No one's could be." Gingerly she gripped the plastic cereal container and placed it on the table. "Well, good morning, Jessie. I'm sorry I scared you."

"Not half as sorry as I am," J.D. said as he levered himself upright. "What on earth made you race into the room like an old polecat was after you?"

"I thought Jessie had been kidnapped...or something."

Amazed, J.D. swung his gaze from Rebecca to the baby and then back again. His mouth opened and closed like a stranded fish. Finally, he jerked a thumb at the messy child. "Who'd want her at the moment? Tell me, so I can call them."

Rebecca choked down a bubble of laugher and grabbed her aching sides. "No, don't get me started again."

J.D. grinned as he considered her. "You aren't serious. Is that really why you—"

"When I found her crib was empty I didn't know what else to think." Except for the suspicions she didn't want to air after seeing him bonding with the child. "At no time could I ever have imagined anything like this."

"I guess you couldn't. Any more than I would have imagined kidnapping. Funny, I wouldn't have thought you that fanciful."

Rebecca ignored that. Before she'd gotten to Texas she wouldn't have, either. "How did you end up feeding Jessie breakfast?"

"I overslept...first time in a long time. When I got up, it was about nine. I heard babbling in her room as I was on my way downstairs. I went in and she wanted to get out. I didn't think it would be such a big deal so I brought her downstairs. I figured Smoke would feed her or something." He scratched his head, then grimaced as he realized his hand was sticky. "But he'd left me a note saying he'd gone out to feed the stock. I opened the door to look for him, but the baby started to fuss so I decided to make her something to eat.'' He sent Jessie an amused look. ''I didn't think it would be so hard. After all, she's got a mouth. You put something in it. Easy as pie.''

That did make Rebecca laugh. ''Oh, right.''

Looking rather sheepish at his naiveté, J.D. rubbed his nose and chuckled. ''Who knew?''

Rebecca smiled in agreement, and confessed, ''I found out the hard way myself the first morning I was alone with her.''

''I guess that cow last night had it a lot easier, huh?''

Laughing, Rebecca nodded. ''I wonder how she's doing this morning?'' She went to the sink to make a bottle for Jessie.

''Fine, I suppose, or Smoke would have come to get me. Why don't we give this little one her milk and go out to see.''

''I think we'd better give her a bath, too…unless you want to carry her around like that?''

J.D. cast his gaze over the baby, now happily trailing her fingers through the sticky glump of cereal all over her tray, then rubbing her hand in her hair. ''Uh…no way. I can meet you—''

Rebecca slapped the warmed bottle into his waving hand. ''Nice try, but I don't think so.''

With a sidelong look, J.D. said, ''What am I supposed to do with this? I've already done my duty this morning.''

''You're going to continue feeding her while I run some bathwater upstairs.'' With one last glance over her shoulder to be certain he was going to follow her direction, she walked to the doorway. Jessie was already babbling and reaching for the bottle. ''Bring her up to the bathroom when you get finished, okay?''

''Reb…Rebecca. Wait a minute. I don't—''

Rebecca chuckled as she walked along the hall, hearing the last of his mutterings die off and the absolute silence that followed. Obviously Jessie was sucking as avidly as those two calves the night before. As she climbed the stairs to the upper hallway, a delighted thrill rippled up Rebecca's spine. It still amazed her to realize what she'd done the night before. And to think she'd never be able to tell anyone back in Boston. Because, quite simply, they wouldn't believe her. Or if they did, they wouldn't understand what the impact had been on her. It was so far out of the realm of most of her friends' and colleagues' experiences, that to try to describe the emotions would have been impossible.

She walked into the bathroom. Last night it had been her refuge, but in the daylight, it was a large, old-fashioned room, painted a sunny yellow. The kind of room one found in old, turn-of-the-century homes. Not like those modern cells they called bathrooms today. There was an old pedestal sink, and a clawfooted tub, with a shower and shower curtain surrounding it on a metal track. She'd noticed last night that the shower curtain had seen better days. Idly, she wondered if she might convince J.D. to get her into town so she could replace it.

Rebecca knelt on the bath mat and turned on the water, allowing it to run onto her wrists to be certain it wasn't too hot for Jessie. What it must be like to give birth, to become a mother. The pride...and the terror, one must feel. Rebecca was sure she'd seen both in that cow's eyes last night. Then she could have kicked herself for allowing her imagination to run riot. She was acting as if she were living in a Disney animal film. She wasn't ordinarily this fanciful. But there was something about Texas. She caught a sight of the view outside the window at the other end of the room. Something about the sweep of the land, the vastness of the sky, the pride and independence that permeated the heated air had crept into her without her even realizing it. There was something about the men too, their strength and passion...no, make that *man*.

Rebecca stared as the man who symbolized Texas to her

walked into the room. J.D. held a contented Jessie tucked into the corner of his arm. But he didn't look satisfied with the cooing baby, he looked like he'd been through a war...or been assaulted by a water balloon. Now he was not only covered with cereal, his shirt was soaking wet, too. The baby on the other hand, looked like the picture of peace and love—if peace and love was a vision that appeared covered with food scraps.

She turned off the tap and stood up. "What happened to you? You look worse than when I left."

"Jessie managed to pull the nipple off the bottle of milk. Before I could get it, she waved her hand and it dumped all over me. So I had to make another one." He scowled as Rebecca laughed. "Next time, you get to feed the kid."

She leaned over and chucked the baby under the chin, smiling as Jessie responded. "Naughty, Jessie. Did you make a mess of Uncle J.D.?"

"Uncle," he said with firm emphasis, "J.D., would like to get out of his nasty clothes." He tried to hand the baby over, but Rebecca backed up.

"You're doing so well, I think you should finish the morning's experience and put her in the tub, too." She giggled. "After all, you're already wet."

J.D. sent her a look that Rebecca could have sworn would start a campfire. "I think...Aunt Rebecca—"

"Oh, I'm not related." Rebecca waved him off. "I'm only temporary, remember?"

"Temporary or not, you're a woman...she's a woman. So I think you should be the one to give her a bath."

Amused, Rebecca placed her hands on her hips. "Are you trying to tell me that a big, tough Texan like you is afraid of seeing—"

"No. I'm not afraid of seeing—"

"—this little female in—"

"—a naked baby." Now totally exasperated, J.D. shifted

the baby and held Jessie out to Rebecca like an offering to appease the gods. "I'm afraid of drowning her!"

To Rebecca's delight, J.D.'s action didn't bother Jessie at all. She just lay there and babbled, suspended in space, and relaxed into the big hands holding her so steadily. Rebecca looked up from his hands—remembering when they weren't so steady, as he had touched her last night. She met his flinty gaze. She knew he could tell what she was thinking when the flint sparked to a tiny flame. Instinctively he brought Jessie close to his chest and cradled her. Rebecca stepped forward. "I'll help you, J.D."

"I...Rebecca..."

"Honest, you can do it."

He frowned, and studied the baby. "Ah, hell."

She started to unbutton the baby's sleeper, only to discover that she was still wearing her soaked diaper from the night before.

"You didn't change her when you got her up?"

"She was already up. It didn't seem to be bothering her none, so I decided not to take a chance."

Rebecca could feel his gaze touch her hair before wandering elsewhere as she busied herself with removing Jessie's clothing. It made her clumsy and she was positive she was blushing. "Jessie seems a remarkably even-tempered child, doesn't she?"

"Considering the family she comes from, I don't know where she gets it."

"Maybe from the father."

"Yeah...maybe."

Rebecca could have kicked herself for bringing that up. She looked up at J.D., but he didn't seem terribly upset, just uncomfortable. "I'm sorry, I didn't mean to—"

"That's okay. It's a fact. Sometimes you gotta face facts, even when you don't want to. Fact is, my sister ran away and somewhere along the line got pregnant. This here baby's the result."

"How do you feel about that, J.D.?" As she waited for the answer, Rebecca's hands continued to strip the wet diaper off, then wad it up and place it across the room in the sink for later disposal.

"I wish… It's not every day a…" he lifted his gaze from the baby and the emotion in his eyes went straight to Rebecca's heart "…a…another…McCoy comes into the world. I wish I could have seen it."

Rebecca walked steadily back to him, feeling as if she were walking into his soul, as if he were suddenly letting her see so much. "You'll see plenty of other McCoys come into this world, J.D. The kind you should be seeing. Your own."

"Well, now, little missy…that takes a mite of loving after you find the right filly."

"Was that a John Wayne imitation? 'Cause if so, that was one of the worst John Wayne imitations I've ever heard." Rebecca knew what he was doing—using humor to avoid getting involved. As a way to back away from her. Just as she'd used uptight prickliness, J.D. used humor. Either that or he left the room. She wouldn't give him a chance to take that option. Besides, Jessie was starting to grumble as her little nude body was held tightly against J.D.'s wet shirt.

J.D. twisted his lips, attempting to make a regretful face. "Shucks, Reb. I never could do John Wayne."

"Well, it doesn't matter. I can't, either." She clapped her hands, trying to seem competent and stay in control. Which was difficult with his grin flashing at her, tempting her to undress him, too. "Time to dump this little one in the tub."

"Dump…"

"I didn't mean it literally, J.D."

"I didn't think you did, darlin'. I may be a simple male in these matters, but I'm not slow." Chuckling, he knelt by the tub and carefully lowered Jessie until she sat like a small Buddha in the shallow water. He moved his head to avoid the baby's delighted splashes, then made a diving grab as one enthusiastic movement made her roll around on her round bottom to tip backward and start to fall. "Whoops, hold on there, cowgirl."

"She loves water. I'm beginning to think she's a duck in disguise," Rebecca added, as she knelt next to him and handed him a washcloth and soap.

"I'm not going to do that. That's your job."

"You're the one who's got hold of her." Rebecca wanted to swoon as she saw those big hands supporting that little body. It was all she could do to concentrate on the bath activity as she saw his lean, tanned fingers against the soft, smooth skin. All she could think of was the power and the tenderness that existed in this man.

"Whoops. Not so's you'd notice," he said, readjusting his grip and grabbing Jessie just as she slipped again on the slick porcelain as she reached for the dangling chain which held the bathtub plug. "This kid is slipperier than Smoke trying to avoid all the widows at the Dewdrop's Friday night dances."

Trying to calm her overactive emotions, Rebecca allowed that comment to divert her from the matter at hand. "Smoke is chased by lonely widows? I thought you were the one with the reputation as a lady-killer."

He reached a hand for the washcloth and dunked it in the water. Squeezing it, he swiped it over the wiggly little body in the water. "I don't know who's been telling you that, but Smoke is right popular with all the 'mature' ladies in town."

"I imagine he is." An image of Smoke, not as she'd first seen him, but as he'd been when he was talking out his worry over J.D., popped into her mind. She bet other women saw the compassion he tried so hard to hide with gruffness, too.

Of course, imagining J.D. as a lady-killer was no stretch

at all. She slid a glance at J.D., who was trying his best to keep Jessie from sucking on the washcloth. Even covered with clumps of drying cereal and smelling like milk standing in the sun on a summer morning, the guy was gorgeous. A beam of morning light highlighted his light brown hair as it curled onto the back of his collar and fell forward around his face, where the gold-tipped strands rested against his cheeks, blazing like sunlight against butter-soft, tanned leather. A shadow from the windowpane fell across his cheekbones, leaving the strong face half mysterious. But all male. His charming grin flashed as he attempted to wrestle the washcloth from the baby who was hanging on to it with both fists. Rebecca wondered how he would look if that were his own baby there in the water, his and—hers.

The notion shook her. As did her rock-solid certainty that she wanted a family. Not just substitutes. Her own. Rebecca wanted to love and be loved. She didn't want to be afraid anymore. To be afraid she was like her mother, setting impossible standards for a man to meet so she didn't have to adapt her own behavior to someone else's expectations. She didn't want to be like her mother, unable to love or share without expecting something concrete in return. As she watched J.D. play with the baby, and saw how far he'd come to accepting this child who had been dumped upon him, she realized the true joy of love is in the giving, not the taking. And she wanted to—

"Reb. Are you all right?"

"Huh?" *Am I all right?* She felt as if she'd just awakened from a long sleep. As if she'd just stepped into the light from a tunnel. Was this what her boss had meant when he'd told her it was time to join the living and look for the hope? What he'd intended she learn when he'd pulled her out of her old position and given her this new one?

"Rebecca…I need a towel."

She blinked. "A towel?"

"To dry off the baby before she turns into a prune."

Looking down, Rebecca was surprised to see a wide-eyed Jessie peering around J.D.'s arm and staring straight up at her. Jessie grinned. For a moment longer, Rebecca stared, then she looked at J.D., thinking she'd never really seen him before.

"Rebecca, what the hell's the matter with you?"

And yet she'd known him in her dreams—not last night's—but in the secret ones that had started "Once upon a time." This was J. D. McCoy, no longer a dream, but the flesh-and-blood man that she wanted in her life. That she never wanted to leave.

"I want to get this kid out of here, so I can wash up and change clothes."

"I'll help you."

He met her gaze then, and the simmering sensuality she saw in response to what must be boiling in her own eyes, thrilled her. "You're going to help me change my clothes? 'Cause if so, you'd better put this baby down for a nap. A long nap. I guarantee we're going to be busy for a long, long time."

At that, Rebecca could feel the heat rush up into her face. She shook her head like a dog leaving a stream and reached for a towel. What on earth was she thinking about? "I'll help with the baby, I mean."

She spread her arms wide as J.D. lifted Jessie up and handed the dripping wet child over to her. Rebecca immediately enveloped her in a big towel, laughing as Jessie tried to pull the terry cloth over her face to play peekaboo with her.

"You'd make a terrific mother, Reb. Ever thought about it?"

Not until I came to Texas. "I haven't had a lot of reason to think about it."

"No steady beau?"

She smiled at the quaint term. "No steady anything."

J.D. helped her to her feet. "Why not?"

"No time, no inclination, no role models. The usual."

J.D. stopped her as she started to walk past him. "Maybe it's time all that changed."

As Rebecca looked up to meet his intense gaze, now deep green in the sunlight, she felt she was standing on the edge of something wonderful...wonderful, thrilling...and terrifying. Her instinct for self-preservation stirred. Regardless of how much she thought she wanted J.D., and how much she discovered having a family and children appealed to her, it was one thing to awaken to the knowledge that these things were important to you, and another thing to leap into the abyss without giving it a lot more thought. And that's what would happen if she followed her desire instead of her head. She knew he wanted her. She knew she wanted him. But as he'd indicated last night, it was all physical for him. At least she could pretend it was for her, too. However, it wouldn't be enough. It couldn't be enough. They were too different. Weren't they? "I don't know."

She wasn't sure if he was disappointed or suddenly relieved that she hadn't responded. Relieved won, she thought. "I have to put some clothes on Jessie."

"Yeah, right. I've got to clean up and get outside."

"See you later."

"Yes...later, maybe." He turned away and went over to the sink. Grimacing, he picked up the soggy diaper and stuffed it in the trash can.

"J.D."

Glancing back, he lifted his brow, but said nothing. He just waited.

She hesitated, then plunged. "If you've got time later today, maybe you could show me some of the ranch and the area?"

He stared at her for a moment before saying, "I could do that, after lunch...I suppose."

Taking a better grip on the squirming baby, she turned

to the door. "After lunch, then. It's a date." Oh, God. Why did she say that?

J.D. winked. "Is it a date?"

She scrambled to preserve something of herself, of the woman she knew. "No. It's just time I saw something of Texas, so I can understand why people love it so. That's all."

"Be careful, Reb. Something about Texas gets in your heart and never lets go. No matter how far away you are."

No kidding, she thought as she backed into the hall.

Something about Texas was already in her heart.

9

J.D. hooked his heel over the railing that enclosed the corral and spoke to Whiskers. "By God, I feel like I've already done a full day's work and all I did was feed that little baby and give her a bath. How in the hell do women do that full-time?" He dug in his pocket and pulled out a carrot. Extending his palm, he offered it to his horse. "No wonder they send us males out to stud. That's the fun part and I'll tell you a secret…" he levered himself up onto the railing, swinging a leg over to sit astride the top "…I'd just as soon keep it that way." That way he wouldn't have to think. He wouldn't have to agonize over his actions, or apologize for his desires—or deal with the result of them, either. Nor would he have had to spend all last night tossing and turning in his lonely bed wanting and worrying about the woman just down the hallway.

"It's gettin' a mite bad when you gotta sit out here talking to some damn horse, boy, 'stead of talking to that good-lookin' filly inside," a familiar voice chided.

"I've just been talking to her." J.D. looked over his shoulder at Smoke, who had just strolled over from the barn to join him. "And now, I've decided to avoid women for a while."

"Why's that?"

"'Cause the more you're with 'em, the more they stick in your mind. That's why." It was the truth. He'd scarcely been able to escape thoughts of Rebecca since she'd arrived. Now after last night, she had somehow twined herself more firmly into his life, so tightly that it was going to be impossible to pry her image from his brain. ''I'm going to remain a bachelor just like you.''

Smoke hung on to the top railing and snorted, sounding very much like Whiskers to J.D. ''I watched you grow up and I never heard such a load of horse manure as you're shovelin' right now. I don't care what you think you think, J.D. You're no more suited to be a bachelor than you can fly. You can't keep this ranch growing if you don't put a family on it. It's time for a woman and some ornery little ones to start running around here and give you what-for when you get outta line. That's just what this place needs.''

''First I've got to find a woman.''

Smoke hit his forehead with the heel of his hand. ''Gawd almighty, if you ain't blind, 'cause I know you ain't stupid!'' He jerked his thumb toward the house. ''What do you call that two-legged creature in there?''

J.D. felt his hackles rise. *Trouble!*

Damn old man. What did he know? Smoke wasn't the one lying awake at night aching for a woman he could never have. Pushing his lower lip out like a stubborn child, he informed Smoke, ''You don't know what the hell you're talking about. Women like Rebecca Chandler don't belong here. They belong in cities, dressed in sophisticated clothes, sipping drinks and smiling at guys with sixty-dollar haircuts. Not sitting on the front porch of a ranch in the middle of nowhere sucking down a beer.'' He started to warm up to the subject. ''And that's all she'd ever get here. You know that. It wouldn't be fair to even say anything.'' He leaned forward, stabbing the air with an aggressive finger. ''Assuming I wanted to say something. Which I don't. So get off my back.''

Like hell he didn't.

If J.D. listened to what his gut was telling him, instead

of trying to rationalize the emotion, he'd grab her and make love to her until neither one of them knew which end was up.

"Excuse me, am I interrupting? Shall I give you two some privacy?"

Both Smoke and J.D. were so involved in their discussion that they hadn't heard Rebecca come up behind them. At her words, J.D. jerked around so rapidly that he had to grab the railing to keep his balance. "Uh…no."

His tongue seemed to be tied in knots as he took in Rebecca standing behind him. He wondered how much she'd heard, but the expression on her face gave nothing away. She gave her cowboy hat a self-conscious tug as she stared back at him. There she stood trying to look at ease, with her trim body all suited up in a pair of jeans that looked like they'd been painted on and a snug top that revealed some of her more womanly attributes. J.D.'s mouth went dry. It was a good thing she was holding the baby, he figured, or he might have ignored everyone and jumped her luscious bones. And rational thought be damned.

Smoke waited for J.D. to say more, but when he didn't, said expansively, "Well, of course you ain't interrupting." He sent J.D. a narrow look. "Fine thing when a body can't walk up to somebody and say howdy without somebody taking offense."

J.D. frowned at Smoke. "I didn't take offense."

"I wasn't talking about you. I was making polite conversation."

Folding his arms, J.D. replied, "You don't know how to make polite conversation."

"Well, as to that, he must be able to, J.D.," Rebecca piped up. "Didn't you tell me that Smoke was quite a hit at the dances on Friday night?"

Smoke sent her a suggestive wink. "Not because of my conversation, missy."

With a reluctant laugh, J.D. agreed. "That's true. He's about the only man who can outdance Edna. Remember, I told you about Edna?"

"She's the one who runs the motel, where you wanted to send us."

With his face set in strong disapproval, Smoke pointed at J.D. "What are you talking about, boy? These two little ladies have to stay right here until your sister comes home."

"That could be a long time comin', Smoke," J.D. said quietly.

"You need to have some trust here, son. I know Rosalie's let you down before, but maybe she growed up some since having this little one." He chucked the baby under the chin, grinning when the baby chuckled.

"What do you think, Re-bec-ca?" J.D. deliberately drawled her name out, trying to see if he could spark some anger or something in her—anything other than this cool, self-possessed exterior she was showing him. That way he wouldn't think about how much he wanted to throw her over his shoulder, mount his horse and ride away with her until he reached a place where he could make love to her all day...and all night. "You're the expert. Has Rosalie grown up?"

Rebecca bit her lip as she looked from one to another. She responded cautiously, "I thought we were making real progress over the last month."

"Progress... Running away and leaving her baby with a stranger is how you define *progress?*" Anything to annoy her and rip her out of his heart—since she seemed so determined to burrow her way in there. The hell of it was, she seemed so good at it.

Rebecca's look nailed him, as if she'd had enough. "I'm not exactly a stranger. And no, I don't call that progress. I call it desperation."

J.D. didn't want to hear that. He didn't like the pictures

the word put into his mind. Telling himself he'd tried his
best to find her didn't help. He forced himself to move.
Throwing his leg over the top railing of the corral, he
shrugged and said, "Whatever you say, Reb. You're the
expert."

Wanting to kick himself for behaving like a sulky infant,
J.D. dropped to the ground on the inside of the fence and
walked over to Whiskers. Grabbing his bridle in his fist, he
turned and walked the horse back to the fence, bringing it
close to Rebecca and the baby. It was time to make amends
and bring the conversation back to normal. J.D. was sick
of making himself miserable, when everything inside him
told him to look for happiness instead.

"Well, now, what do you say to a riding lesson? I'll take
the baby first, then you. How's that sound?"

"That sounds fine. I can't wait," Rebecca responded
with a hearty smile.

Because he hadn't expected her to say that, he was surprised into looking straight at her, finding himself caught
by the determined expression in her blue eyes. "Rebecca,
you surprise me. Aren't you the one who didn't want anything to do with horses?"

"I still don't. I prefer a car."

Smoke laughed. "Can't say I blame you, there. Many's
the time I've spent long hours in the saddle, wishing for a
more comfortable ride. 'Course that's after I've been riding
quite a ways, you understand."

After a sideways glance at Smoke, Rebecca set her jaw.
"Well, comfortable or not, I'm going to ride a horse if it
kills me…or the horse!"

"You're not killing any horses on my ranch, Reb. But
don't worry. It won't come to that. I'm a good teacher."
J.D. mounted Whiskers and brought him alongside the
fence. In her little sunsuit and sun hat, Jessie was a picture.
J.D. grinned as he held an arm out, indicating that Rebecca
place Jessie in it. "Let's see what she does, okay?"

Rebecca hesitated. "Are you sure it's safe? I wouldn't want—"

J.D. cocked a brow and indicated Jessie. "That kid is a McCoy. She was born with ranching blood in her veins. She'll take to it. See if she don't."

Delighted, Jessie started to screech so loudly that Whiskers started to dance in alarm. "Whoa, boy, calm down. She's not going to hurt you." J.D. looked at Rebecca. "Okay, let me have her."

With a dubious expression at the restless horse, Rebecca handed the baby over. J.D. grasped her firmly under her arms and sat her down in the saddle, right in front of him, laughing as Jessie started to babble and rock her body forward and back. "Lookee here, Smoke, this little cowgirl is raring to go."

Smoke's chest thrust out so firmly that you would have thought he'd given birth to the baby himself. "Just like her mother, by gawd! Rosalie was about that little when I put her on a horse in front of your mother."

With a wink at Rebecca, J.D. lay the reins over the horse's neck to turn it to the right. Slowly they walked around, first moving in a big, wide circle before J.D. let Whiskers have a bit more of his head and step out into a trot. As Jessie bounced in front of J.D., the lilting laughter echoed across the corral. "See," he called to Rebecca. "She likes it." So did he. He liked having this little girl in front of him. With only a little effort, J.D. could pretend she belonged to him—really belonged to him. He let himself drift for a moment into a pleasant daydream that promised him a bit of immortality. His arm tightened a bit, as he supported Jessie's warm, round, trusting body. He wanted children. The realization startled him.

Almost reluctantly, J.D. walked the horse back to where Rebecca waited. He dismounted, keeping one hand around the child's waist. "Look at that. She doesn't want to get off." He tried to lift the baby off the horse's back only to discover that Jessie had the horse's mane clenched in her two small fists. Gently J.D. untangled her, laughing at the dissatisfied frown that settled on Jessie's face. "Come on now, let go. Time for your friend to take a ride." He plucked the baby from the horse and turned to hand her to Smoke. He completely ignored Rebecca's outstretched hands. "Ready?"

"I'm not sure I want to get up on that big thing, are you?"

"Rebecca," J.D. sighed. "I just took a six-month-old baby off 'this big thing' and she seemed to do just fine."

"That's because you were with her. You want *me* to get up there all by myself, don't you?"

"That thought did cross my mind, but if you'd prefer I can take you for a ride, too." Suddenly he found more enthusiasm for the idea when he realized that he would have that curvy little posterior nestled against him.

Rebecca must have read his mind, because she blurted, "Is that the horse you would ordinarily teach someone to ride on?" Then she sent Whiskers, who was pulling at the reins in J.D.'s hands, a narrow look. "Isn't there a nice gentle old horse? Not one so high-spirited?"

Smoke chortled. "Dang if she don't have a point, J.D. How about we get Lightning out and let Rebecca give her a go?"

J.D. sent Smoke a funny look before sending Rebecca a speculative glance. "Lightning? Do you think she can handle her?"

"Lightning doesn't sound too good to me," Rebecca said. "Don't you have a Rheumatism or Rocking Chair, or something?"

"Nope." J.D. rubbed his chin thoughtfully. "I agree with Smoke. I think it had better be Lightning. If you can't learn to ride Lightning you aren't fit to spend time in Texas."

"God," Rebecca muttered, "you make Texas sound like a mental institution."

J.D. laughed. "You stay right here now, Reb. I'll be right back." He raced over to the barn and reemerged with a horse in record time.

"Here comes Lightning," Smoke announced.

Blinking, Rebecca finished reciting the Twenty-third Psalm. She lifted her hands over her brows, shading her eyes to get a better look at the horse in question. "That's Lightning?"

To J.D. the look on her face was priceless. "None other," he agreed as he led the horse over to the railing. He bit back a smile as he watched Rebecca take in the calm, almost catatonic demeanor of the horse. If there was a horse anymore laid back than Lightning, J.D. didn't know where he'd find it. "Rosalie named her Lightning because she is the calmest, most gentle horse we have. My sister didn't want her to feel bad about not being more...dynamic."

"That girl has the devil's own sense of humor," Smoke agreed.

"Yeah," Rebecca said, dryly, "sort of like her brother."

"Climb on up here Reb and I'll show you the slowest ride in all of Texas."

Rebecca clambered over the fence. Awkwardly, she climbed down the other side. "These jeans are a bit tight."

J.D. had been appreciating the sight since she walked up to the corral. "I know."

She gave him a suspicious look. "I didn't bring any, so I had to borrow these and the hat from Rosalie's room, so I'd be more appropriately dressed." She blew the hair away from her face with an annoyed gesture. "Anyway, they must have been hers when she was younger."

"You fill them out a bit better than Rosalie did." Had she intended to ride all along? he wondered. Had she decided to give him a hard time for a while to go along with the one he was giving her? He sent her a sideways glance. Would this woman ever stop surprising him?

Self-consciously she slid her hands down her thighs. "I, uh…"

"Well," Smoke announced, as he squinted up at the sky. "Lord almighty knows, it's gonna be a scorcher today. You two can stay out here in the sun if you want." He wiped his brow. "Best I get this young'un inside, though. I got me some string beans to snap for dinner, and then I've got a ton of other inside chores so I can take care of this little one for the rest of the day." Smoke smiled as his gaze gently touched them both. "You two go ahead and take your time."

To J.D., Smoke's smile was almost maternal—that is, if his mother had been a wizened, old cowboy with a huge hat and a semitoothed smile. The thought of Smoke playing cupid amused J.D. as much as it annoyed him. When would this pesky old man stop butting into his life? Before he could say anything, though, Smoke had turned on his heel and marched toward the ranch house. J.D. rubbed his chin as he watched his old friend and mentor stomp up the steps onto the back porch. J.D. sent Rebecca a sheepish smile. "Smoke seems to think we should spend some time alone together."

Suddenly amused, Rebecca nodded. "So I see."

"Subtle, isn't he?"

"Like a two-ton boulder in an avalanche."

Chuckling, J.D. agreed. Then he eyed Lightning before looking back to focus on Rebecca. "Fact is, nobody should leave Texas without taking a horseback ride in the countryside."

"How about a ride in the corral instead?"

"You said you wanted to see some of the land. So, I think we'll get you up on old Lightning here and just mosey on that way." He waved toward the open range that stretched far beyond the enclosed paddocks. "We'll go as far as those hills, just over there and then come on back."

"That's pretty far." Doubt crept over her face as she nibbled her bottom lip. "Well, I can try. However, my riding skills—"

J.D. reached over the railing and took her hand in his, marveling at how soft it felt against the hard calluses on his palm. "Relax, Reb. I won't let anything hurt you." He wished he could be as sure about her thinking the same.

Rebecca stared at him for a moment, then withdrew her hand and climbed back over the fence to stand to the side of the horse. She reached out and gave Lightning a tentative pat. When the horse only flicked her eyes in her direction, Rebecca asked, "Do you think she minds that I touched her? I mean, she felt that didn't she?"

Laughing, J.D. responded as he grabbed her by the waist and practically threw her into the saddle. "Honey, since you're going to be sitting on top of her for a while, she'd better not mind." He decided the shock tactic of putting her on the horse instead of helping her learn to mount was the best thing. Besides, it gave him an excuse to put his hands on her. He'd been dying to do that since she came outside.

Rebecca grabbed the saddle horn to regain her balance before she slipped off the other side. Awkwardly she straightened and grabbed the reins, surprising the horse with the motion. At least, J.D. thought, she would have surprised Lightning if the horse had been capable of so strong an emotion.

To J.D.'s utter amusement, Rebecca sat like a piece of antique china while he walked into the corral, mounted Whiskers and led him out of the gate.

"Ready, Reb?"

Only Rebecca's eyes moved, as she asked, "Do I say giddy-up or something?"

J.D. bit his lip to keep the laughter inside. God, this

woman was adorable. A prickly pear on the outside and a mass of sweet fruit on the inside. He couldn't remember when he'd last been so amused by a female.

"You have to put her in gear and say the magic words."

"What are the magic words?"

J.D. leaned over and whispered into the horse's ear. Rebecca squeaked as Lightning started to move.

"Good Lord, what did you say to her?"

J.D. allowed his horse to pace by Lightning as they moved down the road. "It's a cowboy secret, darlin'. I'll tell you before we come back."

"I hope so, or I might end up in Park for the duration of the ride."

J.D. led the way toward the far pastures and the hills behind. He glanced at Rebecca. "You're doing real well. Have you been on a horse before?"

"Twice, when I was a kid. Husband number two—or was it three?—liked horses. But one day the guy was being a real jerk, so I vowed never to get up on one again." Rebecca glanced over at him, her face carefully blank and chillingly remote. "He liked horses more than kids, you see. So, the only way I could make an impact was to refuse to do what he wanted me to do so badly."

"I see." And he did. With that one statement, Rebecca Chandler had put her entire childhood into perspective for him. Plus, she'd illuminated the strength of will that made her able to tackle anything she wanted and be successful. That was an intriguing concept to J.D., although he was afraid to explore why more deeply. So, he only smiled and they continued to ride on in silence.

A hot, very hot, while later, J.D. stopped his horse and looked around at the stand of trees which led down to the river. "I wanted you to see this. My favorite spot when I was growing up is right around here." Try as he might to stop it, he kept inviting her closer to him. He wanted her to share the things that meant the most to him.

"Your favorite spot?" Rebecca shifted in the saddle and used the hem of her top to wipe her dripping brow. "Lord, it's hot. Is it always this hot?"

"Yep," J.D. acknowledged with a strangled sound as he stared, mesmerized by the soft stretch of skin she'd revealed, which extended from right below her breasts to her waist. He reached for his ever-present kerchief and lifted his hat to swipe his forehead. "Mighty hot." He wished he were talking about the weather. "Summer's really settling in."

"How do you stand it?"

J.D. pursed his lips as he considered her. Then he made up his mind. "I'm about to show you, darlin'." He dismounted and dropped the reins so Whiskers would stand without moving, then turned to lift a surprised Rebecca off her horse. Grabbing the reins of both horses in one hand and Rebecca's hand in the other, he led them through the trees until they came to—

"Is that a pond?" Rebecca exclaimed, tugging at J.D.'s hand.

"Not exactly. It's a swimming hole, made by a freshwater stream that eventually flows into the river."

"I'd like to stick my hands in it and cool my face a bit."

After giving her a wicked look, J.D. tied the horses to a bush and turned to face her. "Honey, we're going to stick more than our hands in that water."

Rebecca looked longingly at the rippling pond, then down at her clothes. "I wish I'd worn my swimming suit."

J.D.'s grin widened. "You don't need a suit."

"I certainly do. I don't want to get my clothes all wet." Rebecca plucked at her pants leg. "These jeans are tight enough dry. Wet, they'd really be uncomfortable."

J.D. stared at Rebecca, as she stood there, self-conscious in her tight blue jeans. She might not be comfortable in the clothing she wore, but, J.D. thought, they suited her. She probably wouldn't believe him if he said so. However,

those jeans suited her independent spirit and the noncon-
forming nature Rebecca generally hid under her polished
exterior. These clothes suited the woman inside. And the
woman inside suited J.D., right down to the ground, regardless of what he'd said to Smoke earlier. But he wasn't
certain how to tell her. He didn't want her to take pity on
him, considering him something she'd always remember as
her big Western adventure. Instead, J.D. wanted to make
Rebecca look at him, and see only him—Jesse Delaney
McCoy. A man who wanted her. A man who could help
her realize how special she was.

He hesitated. For a moment he felt inadequate, like the
iron-jawed man of few syllables she'd expected him to be.
He didn't know if he had the words to explain—besides
words always seemed to get them in trouble—but he could
definitely show her how he felt.

"Darlin'," he said slowly, "you're about to discover the
best part about living out in the middle of nowhere."

Her brows lifted, with a suspicious arch. "Which is…?"

J.D. tossed his hat aside and stripped off his shirt. His
hands were unbuckling his belt as he answered, "Skinny-
dipping."

Rebecca's eyes grew so wide and round, J.D. could
swear they encompassed the world. Or was he confusing
her eyes with the world? Damned if he knew. All he was
sure of was, he needed to see her, touch her, and try to
convince her she would love it here if she gave it a chance.
All she had to do was apply that formidable willpower to
being happy in Texas.

"I can't possibly…"

J.D. pulled off his boots, and yanked off his socks. Then
he unzipped his fly, noticing that she'd stopped protesting.
Instead—

Rebecca couldn't take her eyes off of him. She tried to
force herself to look away, but it took more willpower than
she could muster to pull her gaze from his lean, rippling

muscles covered with all that smooth, bronzed skin. Her look touched his chest, the mat of hair a light brown tipped by gold to match the streaks in his hair. Rebecca was sure he spent long hours working out in the sun with his shirt off. Unable to help herself, her eager gaze followed the straight line of his hair that formed a directional arrow to one of his more interesting areas. The area now being revealed by the rasping slide of the zipper on his jeans. She wet her lips. "J.D.—"

His fingers didn't pause as he answered, "Hmm?" Instead, he hooked his thumbs in his waistband and forced the worn material down lower on his hips, then down onto his legs. With one smooth movement he stepped out of his jeans.

He stood at ease, the stark white of his cotton underwear contrasting with his tan. Rebecca wasn't surprised to see the power hidden by his clothing, but she was surprised to see he wore not conventional jockey shorts, but very low-cut briefs. They reminded her of the suits worn by competition swimmers, except for some obvious differences of course, like the slit in front which tempted her to slide her hand inside to see if what was hidden under the cloth was as tempting as what was promised. Reminding herself to breathe, she let the pent-up heat escape as she exhaled. Without being aware of making a conscious decision she started to unbutton her own top. It was only a swim, she told herself.

She couldn't take her eyes from his as he waited...and watched. With an abandonment she would have sworn she could never possess, she tossed her hat aside, then slid her fingers under the hem of her shirt and lifted. As she pulled the shirt over her head and flung it after the hat, she could feel her breasts in their lacy bra beginning to burn from the intensity of his gaze. She took a deep breath to unbutton the top of her tight jeans, then tried to push them down. Naturally they promptly got stuck because they were too small for her. So much for her dreams of shedding her clothing as if she were a seductive siren, accustomed to this sort of activity.

His voice shook slightly as he asked, "Need any help?"

Rebecca looked up to see him standing closer, bending solicitously over her with one corner of his mouth lifting in an appealing, quirky grin. "Rosalie must have been a lot smaller when she got these jeans. Or else I somehow gained five pounds on our ride."

"Trust me, your body is absolutely delicious—even if you gained some, which you didn't. Don't fret, darlin', it's the heat. Your body's a bit sticky, that's all."

Rebecca gasped as his palms brushed the outside of her legs, before slipping to the inside of her thighs to help her pull the seams down. Suddenly shy, she pushed his hands away. "I can get it, thanks." Wiggling her hips she managed to get the jeans down, only to have them stick on her low-heeled ankle boots. Before she could bend to take care of the problem, J.D. was kneeling at her feet, lifting her leg to remove first one shoe, then the other. When he looked up at her and smiled, Rebecca grabbed at his shoulders to keep her balance—or so she told herself—not because she wanted to touch him. He skimmed his hands up the sides of her body as he rose. Taking her hands in his, J.D. stepped back to look at her.

Rebecca flushed, even though she was as fully covered as she would be if she was wearing a bikini. It wasn't the amount of coverage, but the fact that her bikini and bra were actually bought as underwear that she found disconcerting. "I...maybe..."

"Shhh," J.D. said in a drawl as smooth as warm honey. "Just relax, Rebecca. Nothing's going to happen here that you don't want to happen. We're going swimming, that's all."

No, that wasn't all, Rebecca thought. What was really happening was that she was afraid she was falling in love with the long, tall Texan standing in front of her. And that was definitely something she didn't want to happen. Unfortunately, it might be too late.

Rebecca allowed him to lead her toward the water, then shivered as he continued to walk forward. The cool liquid played with her aroused senses like a mirage to a thirsty man, tempting her to abandon all inhibitions, to let the current take her wherever it might.

It took her right into his open arms.

As his arms closed around her, she felt herself submerge in the deeper water until her entire body cooled, the heat of the day only a memory. Then another type of heat began when her legs and hips floated forward and tangled with his as he backed into deeper water. Awkwardly, she tried to untangle them.

"Oops, sorry…I haven't been swimming for a while."

His touch soothed her as much as his voice. "Hush now, darlin', everything's okay. This little ole swimming hole isn't deep until you get to the center."

"We're in deep enough as it is." She wasn't talking about the water.

"I know," he said with an understanding look. "And it's too late to go back. Why don't we just relax and go where it takes us?"

She felt every muscle in her body release. She let herself go with the flow. With the flow of the water around her, and with the flowing, internal rhythm that was as old as time, as demanding as existence. A new tension began when her breasts touched his chest. The wet, thin nylon made it seem as if she were wearing nothing at all—a fact she knew he was well aware of, as his desire started to swell. Following her instincts, her legs lifted to encircle his hips. Or had he lifted them? As her lips met his, she wasn't sure. Nor did she care. She opened her mouth, greedy to taste him. As greedy to taste as she was to experience. Her lips slanted across his and her tongue invaded, tangling fiercely with his, wanting more, needing more, her probing kisses becoming hotter, deeper. Her hips arched against him, feeling the exquisite tingle that indicated her womanhood. Aroused, she pressed kisses all over his face and finished by licking the water from his neck, enjoying the slight raspy feeling of his beard, before he growled and took her mouth again.

Aggressively his hands slid behind her back to unfasten her bra. He slipped the straps over her arms, allowing the garment to fall forward and remain caught between their bodies before the water claimed it. Frantically he lifted her in his arms, lifting her above him so he could taste her breasts. She placed her hands on his shoulders to give his mouth better access. Rebecca moaned as J.D.'s teeth teased her nipple. She groaned as his mouth continued to suck her sensitive breasts. All around her she felt the water, the cradle of life, the nurturer of Mother Earth, and was stunned at the elemental force and power that invaded her as her desire mounted. Unable to wait, she thrust her fingers into his hair and yanked his mouth up to hers, resting her arms on his shoulders.

"Touch me, J.D.," she whispered.

He needed no more urging. He cupped her buttocks, before sliding one hand around her hips to remove the wet bikini that still covered her. She jerked as his fingers found her, relaxing into his embrace before impatience overcame her.

"I need to touch you, too."

"Be my guest, darlin'."

J.D. pushed her hand down, well below the water. She found him, the buoyancy of the water making it difficult to keep her balance. She slid her hand inside the opening of his briefs and caressed him for a moment before impatiently tugging at the fabric, trying to pull them off. He helped her.

Then they were free.

Her hand encircled him and she gasped at his size. She

licked her lips and smiled. "Everything in Texas is larger than life, isn't it?"

He grinned. "And ready for action, darlin'."

With that, his fingers slid into her, helping to bring the liquid heat of her desire to the surface, where it could melt with the ripples around her. The water seemed to heat as his fingers continued to caress her. She was aware of every drop, of every brilliant glimmer of light on the small waves that lapped around them as they moved. She ravaged him with her lips, teeth and tongue before spreading her legs wide, allowing him to ravage her in turn. He slipped inside, an inch at a time, until she was certain it would last forever. With each push forward the now warm water advanced until she felt heat, inside and out. As he started to move, she threw her head back to glance at the sky, the deep blue above her. Rebecca let the sun bake into her until she felt as liquid as a puddle, dissolving into the water lapping around their hips. As the heat increased, she opened her heart to the expanse of Texas and the only man in it for her, well aware that once she did, life would change. She could never go back. But that didn't matter, as long as she continued to go forward. As long as he continued to go forward with her and finish what they'd started.

Damn, she was so tight, J.D. thought. He'd never felt anything like this before. If he didn't know better, he'd swear she was a virgin. Then he started to lose it as her body clenched around him. After that, rational thought evaporated as he pushed deeper, feeling each convulsive movement as his sensitive member pressed forward. It wouldn't be long before he wouldn't be able to control himself. He didn't want to control himself. He wanted to explode. He had to explode. He was determined to let his passion climb to the wide-open Texas sky and take her with him, until she became as much a part of Texas as she was becoming part of him.

"J.D., now, please now. I can't wait any longer."

"Me, either," he gasped. "Hang on darlin', dig your heels in now, 'cause I'm going to take you for the ride of your life." He did. And in exchange she rode him to a standstill, until the power spurted out of him, mixing with the liquid in her and around her. Until there was no more power left in either of them.

There was only satisfaction as they sank down into the water.

Moments later they surfaced. J.D. shook the wet hair from his eyes. "Rebecca, darlin' are you all right?"

Rebecca blinked her eyelashes rapidly, to clear her eyes of water. "I think so."

"I wasn't trying to drown us, darlin'. My knees buckled right there at the end and I—"

Rebecca placed her fingers over his mouth. "Shhh. It was wonderful."

Still holding her, with her legs still wrapped tightly around him, he stepped into more shallow water. And reluctantly felt their contact break. She lowered her legs to stand in front of him. As beautiful in the sunlight as that portrait of the goddess rising from the sea that he'd seen in books. Aphrodite, goddess of love, that's who it was. Focusing on Rebecca's alabaster skin which gleamed in the light, he thought the analogy was appropriate. She glowed with love in the strong afternoon sun. He wanted her again. He led her from the pond, grabbing their undergarments from the water, and stepped to his horse to remove a blanket. Spreading it on the ground along with their wet clothes, he turned and held out his hand. "Come over here darlin', we'll let that good old Texas heat dry us off."

Smiling, she stepped toward him and allowed him to take her hands and pull her down. Quickly he rolled her over onto her back.

"J.D.," she exclaimed, laughing, "what are you doing?"

"Making love to you. On dry land this time." His lips touched hers. "Any objections?"

"Suppose someone were to—"

"No one will. It's just you, me, the horses, the sky above and the earth below."

Rebecca smiled, a soft, come-hither smile that set his pulse beating in triple time. "Sounds like quite a crowd."

Lazily, J.D. let his hand wander over her body. "We could be in the middle of the Astrodome and I'd still make love to you."

Rebecca chuckled. "You know what?"

"What?"

"I wouldn't care a bit." Then she pulled him on top of her, spreading wide to allow him access to her pleasure. She gripped his buttocks and with a fierce moan, urged him to get inside her. "Love me, J.D. Right here on this Texas soil that you're so much a part of."

Without another word, J.D. did.

10

_____◄─►_____

The light was sinking toward the west when they finally arrived back at the ranch. Still unable to keep from touching her, J.D. lifted Rebecca off Lightning and kept a tight hold of her hand as he led both horses into the stables. "We have to unsaddle them and rub them down." Then he gave Rebecca a wry look. "Not that they had to work very hard this afternoon."

"Oh, I don't know." Rebecca sent him a sideways look from under her lashes. "Lightning and Whiskers must have sweated horribly out there in the sun for a good part of the afternoon."

Smiling, J.D. agreed. "Yeah, it was pretty hot." He lifted her hand to his cheek for a brief caress, then released it to unsaddle the horses.

"Oh, it was. Positively steamy, I'd say."

"You would, huh? Why Rebecca Chandler, I'm ashamed of you."

"You are?"

J.D. grabbed her and kissed her. "Absolutely."

Silently, he handed Rebecca a brush and they started currying the horses. As they worked, J.D. tried to think of the best way to ask the question that had been bothering him all afternoon. "Rebecca, when we were making love...I could have sworn, that is...well..."

Rebecca avoided his eyes, instead concentrating fiercely on smoothing the brush over Lightning's hide.

Finally, lacking a tactful way to put it, he blurted, "Rebecca, are you a virgin?"

Blushing, Rebecca looked at the ground for a moment, before throwing back her shoulders and turning to face him. She lifted her chin. "Not anymore."

J.D. staggered back against the stall. "But—but, you couldn't have been. I mean, you're how old?" All the way back to the ranch, he'd kept telling himself that he was totally nuts to consider it. He'd sworn his desire had overwhelmed him, until he didn't know what he felt, physically or emotionally. That's why his imagination had taken over and made her a virgin.

"I don't think my age is the issue. Surely I'm not the world's oldest living virgin!" With an exasperated look, Rebecca continued, "Regardless of what you think."

"I didn't mean to suggest that. It's just—well, you've got to admit it's damn unusual." Then, he turned around. "What the hell is the matter with the men in Boston?"

"Maybe it's because they're in Boston."

"Cold fish, you mean?"

"No…no, that's not fair." Rebecca shook her head. "It wasn't them. It was me. I'd watched my mother and the men she'd known—the men she'd married. I decided that wasn't how I wanted to live my life." She lifted her chin, proudly. "I was going to be more selective."

Letting herself out of the enclosure, she led her horse to a stall and put her inside. After she slid the lock behind the animal, Rebecca turned and started to pace, seeming to think aloud as she tried to explain herself. "Unlike my mother, I don't see sex as a weapon or a tool, J.D. It should be more than that. It should mean something. Not be merely pure physical satisfaction. I decided that I wouldn't give myself to someone unless I was in love. Unless it meant everything in the world to me." She stopped and glanced over her shoulder before looking away, as if stricken by what she'd said.

"Everything—" J.D. marched from the stall and grabbed her shoulders. He whirled her around to face him. "Are you saying what I think you're saying? 'Cause if you are, it's—it's—" He wasn't sure how he should respond. He was probably making a mess of this entire situation, but he didn't know how to act. How to explain his feelings.

"It's what?"

"Pretty damn scary, that's what it is. And I don't—"

"I see," Rebecca interrupted him. "Well, that makes your position perfectly clear, doesn't it?"

"I don't know what my position is." At the moment, reality was all mixed up with dreams, then confused by fear. He released her shoulders and stepped back. J.D. lifted his hat and shoved his fingers though his hair before jamming the hat back onto his head. "I mean, here you are, one minute a sophisticated woman of the world, the next a green girl. I don't mind the woman. But I'm not sure I want the responsibility for the girl."

"You don't mind the woman," Rebecca repeated slowly. For a moment she stared at him, then exhaled with a long, uneven breath. She stabbed a finger in his direction. "Regardless of what you think, J. D. McCoy, I'm no green girl. You have no responsibility for me. I'm responsible for myself."

"Of course I'm responsible for you. You're on my land, under my roof. Hell, you were even *under* me." He slammed the heel of his hand against his forehead. "Oh, damn me for a ham-handed fool—I didn't even use a condom. What the hell was I thinking of?" He sent her an appalled look. "You could be pregnant right now."

"Don't worry. If anything happens, it's none of your business."

"Don't be ridiculous. It is, too, my business."

"Not anymore than your sister's pregnancy was, after she ran away."

"If I'd known about that little episode of Rosalie's, it would have ended up differently."

"Well, you didn't. So, lucky you—now you get a second chance to help by taking them in, and providing a home."

"That's not the point, Rebecca. Don't try to change the subject. You—"

"Oops, excuse me. Is this private? Should I leave?" A curious feminine voice interrupted them, then chuckled as she looked around. "What is it about these stables, J.D.? Every time you're in them, you're arguing with a woman. First me, then poor Rebecca."

"Rosalie." J.D. stood as if struck by lightning.

"Well, at least you didn't forget what I look like."

J.D. felt all the blood leave his brain as he stared at his sister. Was she real? Or had he conjured her up? Had fate decided to play a trick on him by bringing her back to the scene of their last encounter? He squeezed his eyes shut, keeping them tightly closed for a second. When J.D. opened them, Rosalie was still there.

The nervous tremble of her lips was immediately controlled by a forced grin as she shrugged her shoulders and said, "I wouldn't blame you if you had."

J.D. came to life and stepped forward. Forget what she looked like? It would be like looking into a mirror and trying to forget himself. She was still the image of him, but smaller, younger, blonder...and now older. Where there had been round-faced youth, there was now finely drawn maturity. It was completely disconcerting, and yet so typically Rosalie, to surprise him. *Damn her.*

"Where did you come from? What the hell are you doing here?" Balling his hands into fists, he shoved them into his pockets. He had to, or he would have tried to strangle her— after he'd hugged her to death first. God, she looked good to him. He'd missed her.

"I came from Nashville. And I've come to get my baby, of course. Where else would I be?"

"Knowing you, I haven't the vaguest idea. I didn't expect it to be here, though." The acid tone in his voice made his sister flinch. Then to J.D.'s surprise, she threw her shoulders back and tossed her head. She stood there looking like the old Rosalie, determined to take her medicine. But not about to give an inch more than necessary.

"Well, that's honest. And unfortunately, I deserve it." She moistened her lips. "J.D., I want to apologize for—"

J.D. held up his hand. "I'm not the one you should be apologizing to at the moment. I think you owe Rebecca more of one."

At that, Rosalie turned to face the woman standing outside the stall, next to J.D. "I owe Rebecca everything."

"Are you all right, Rosalie?" Rebecca asked, quietly.

Rosalie nodded. "I am now. Thanks to you."

Placing his fists on his hips, J.D. said, "Well, you're not going to be all right when I get my hands on you. I'm going to turn you over my knee and wail the living tar out of you."

Lifting her chin in her old pugnacious manner, Rosalie responded, "Oh, you think so, do you? That's exactly like you, J.D. I haven't seen you in three years, and what do you do? You threaten to beat my butt first thing. You were always threatening to beat my butt."

"Just threatening?" Rebecca questioned, darting a look at them both.

J.D. sent Rebecca an outraged glance. *What did she think he was—some kind of abuser?* Then he surprised himself, as he felt his mouth split into a wide grin. "I don't blame you for asking, Reb. But, truth was, I couldn't catch her most of the time. That kid was faster than a greased piglet when it came to saving her hide. She led me quite a chase, nine times out of ten."

Grinning back, Rosalie said, "It was worth it to see you

running around waving that old pancake turner of Mom's. Telling me how you'd smash me into a patty when you got hold of me.'' She reached her hand forward and caressed her brother's cheek. ''The way I remember it now, you never did catch me, did you?''

He covered her hand with his, and swallowed the lump in his throat as he tried to talk. ''Sure I did. But somehow I couldn't bring myself to blister your little behind, once I had the chance.''

Rebecca stepped around the two of them. ''If you'll both excuse me, I think the two of you have some issues to resolve. I'll see you inside, later.''

Reaching out to stop her, J.D. grabbed her arm. ''Wait a minute. You and I have things to discuss, too, Reb.''

''No, we don't.'' Rebecca shook herself free. ''You made yourself perfectly clear a moment ago. And truthfully, I need to pack. It's time to go home.''

''Go home? You're going to go home?'' He snapped his fingers. ''Just like that.''

Imitating his snap, Rebecca said, ''That's right. Just like that.'' She indicated Rosalie. ''My job here is over.''

''What about your vacation?'' J.D. fought to keep down the panic that started to rise at the thought of her leaving. But Rebecca only shrugged as he continued. ''You can still stay here on the ranch, or in Wildwalk if you'd prefer.''

''I've decided to go to Paris instead. I haven't been there in a while.'' Rebecca gave him a cool smile, barely a quirk of the lips. ''I think a sophisticated city jaunt suits me better than a one-horse town in Texas, don't you?''

J.D. stared at her. The reality of the gulf between them suddenly slammed him in the gut. After a moment, his lips twisted. ''I reckon you're right, Miss Chandler.'' The words had a sour taste as he watched her leave the barn. Damn, he thought, what happened here?

''I'll be there in a little bit, Rebecca,'' Rosalie called.

"Take your time," Rebecca answered over her shoulder as she continued walking.

J.D. avoided Rosalie's eyes when she turned to him and asked, "What's going on, J.D.?"

He wasn't sure he could tell her. This afternoon he could have sworn this was the woman he wanted by his side forever. Now— The sudden destruction of his dreams was too much for him to cope with at the moment. So, he attacked instead. "How in the holy hell did you have the nerve to walk off and leave your baby on that woman's doorstep? Then, send me a note, telling me to take care of her. How did you know I'd even be here?"

"Were else would you be?" Rosalie's eyebrows shot up in astonishment. "You're a McCoy. This is McCoy land. You'd die if you had to leave it."

"There are worse things than leaving the land," J.D. said, looking in the direction of the barn door, through which Rebecca had disappeared moments before. *There's loving…and losing.*

"You're right, J.D. I discovered that."

J.D. pulled his attention back to his sister. "Rosalie, I didn't mean it when I told you to get out if you weren't happy here. I never meant for you to leave. I…I said it 'cause I was frustrated, not because—"

Rosalie placed her hand over J.D.'s mouth. "J.D., shhh. It wasn't anything you said. I was an idiot. A young, foolish idiot."

He pulled her hand away. "If you hate it here, you don't have to stay. I can help you and the baby get a place somewhere else. I know it's not much here and—"

"J.D., stop. Don't you talk about the ranch that way. This is home. My roots are here and I'll always love it. I didn't realize how much until I left it." She walked over to touch one of the big beams that supported the barn. Stroking it lovingly, she said, "When I ran away, it was only because I thought there was something better out there. For me, at least. It took me a long time to find it, and then, I found it only because I wasn't looking for it.''

"You mean the baby?"

"Partly. The baby, and the baby's father, Tim."

"Tim, who?"

"Tim Enderwine. He's a country-and-western singer, from Texas, believe it or not. But he's playing guitar and singing backup with a country star, at the moment."

"A musician? Was he the one dragging you all over the countryside?" Frowning, he scratched his head. "You were really involved with a musician?" Although, if he had to picture Rosalie with the complete opposite of any of the young cowboys she'd flirted with as a kid, a musician sure fit the bill. Even a cowboy sort of musician from Texas.

"I know what you're thinking—musicians are unsteady, egotistical, restless.... I mean, I told him I didn't want anything to do with a musician right after I met him. I was so horrible to him, that after a time, he finally accepted it. He left me and went to Nashville."

"He left you and the baby? What kind of guy is this?"

"He didn't know about the baby. I didn't tell him, until recently."

An image of Rebecca flashed into J.D.'s mind. It was exactly what she'd threatened to do if she was pregnant. Nope—he damn well wouldn't wait until his child was six months old before he found out about it. "Even so—"

"I married him, J.D."

Stunned, J.D. could only stare at her.

"Rebecca advised me to search out my dreams and not stop until I'd made them come true. So, I tracked him down and married him. Yesterday, in Nashville."

"You what? Why would you want to do that?" Confused, J.D. looked around the barn, looking for answers. "You just said this was your home. It's where you belong. You're back now."

"Oh, J.D., much as I've discovered how much I love the

ranch, and the land, and you—I love him more. I love him so much that I'd give up anything for him. He needs to be in Nashville, for his career.''

''But—''

''J.D., it's time for me to leave home for good. Not just run away, like I did before.'' Rosalie started to cry. ''I'm so sorry for how I've hurt you. I was such a selfish little—''

''Hush now, brat.'' J.D. took her into his arms and held her close. After the last three years of pain and guilt, he thought he'd never be able to forgive her—much less himself. It was amazing to discover how easy it was. How it freed him to look to the future. His future.

He kissed her hair. ''It's going to be all right, brat. Who knows, maybe I even deserved some of it. I could be an arrogant, humorless bastard sometimes.'' He chuckled as he reached for his handkerchief to dry Rosalie's eyes. ''Then again, you could be a real pain in the ass! But mad as I was at you, I hated to think of you in trouble...or on the streets.''

''It wasn't that bad, J.D. I didn't have to do anything you'd be ashamed of. Actually, I worked with a rodeo for quite a while, working with the horses. That's how I got around the country, after I left L.A. The rodeo is where I first met Tim. He was in a band, who played some gigs with the show for a while.''

''A rodeo?'' Astonished, J.D. stepped back and looked at her. ''Damn. I never thought of checking rodeos.''

''I guess not.'' Rosalie grinned. ''Not after what I said about horses and ranches and the like.''

''Is that how you got to Boston?''

''Yep. I was about six months pregnant when we got there. I was afraid of the strenuous work I'd been doing. So, I decided I needed another job. One of the girls in the rodeo helped me get into the system. You know, sign up for unemployment and find a place to stay, and all.''

''And, that's how you met Rebecca?''

"Yeah. I'd never met anyone like Rebecca before."

"Me, either." *And I don't think I ever will again.* He suddenly realized letting go of his anger left him more room in his heart for love.

"J.D., come inside with me. I want you to meet Tim. He's in there getting acquainted with the baby. We've been here most of the afternoon."

"You go on in. I'll be along in a minute, okay?"

"Okay." Rosalie threw her arms around her brother and gave him a kiss. "God, J.D. It's so good to see you. I've missed you so much."

"Get along with you. Go try your charm on Smoke."

"I already have," Rosalie grinned.

"Where'd it get you?"

"It got me a fresh batch of Smoke's stovetop brownies."

Grinning, J.D. nodded. "He always had a soft spot for you. Now me, I still get the hard-as-a-cow-chip biscuits."

Rosalie sent him a saucy wink over her shoulder as she left the barn. "If you're really nice, I'll share."

"Make sure you do. I still have that pancake turner of Mom's around somewhere. And I'm willing to bet age has slowed you down some."

Stopping, Rosalie turned and slid a look from the top of J.D.'s hat to the bottom of his boots. "Back at ya, big brother. Although, I do think age becomes you. You're even better looking than I remembered. Has Rebecca noticed?"

"Nice try brat, but I still want some of your brownies."

"Damn." Rosalie chuckled, whirled on her heel and sailed out the barn.

J.D. moved to the door and leaned against the wide frame, resting his shoulder comfortably against the wood as he watched his sister enter the house. "Rosalie married," he whispered. That was almost as earth-shattering as Rosalie with a baby. He wished he could make time stand still. If he could, his mom and dad would still be alive. And

who knows where he'd be—he and Rosalie. Maybe he'd
even be living in a city. Maybe he would have left the ranch
and found another career. Maybe he would have run into
Rebecca at the opera. No, not the opera, he didn't like
opera—at least he didn't think he did. Did Rebecca?

There was so much he didn't know about her. He didn't
know her favorite color. Or what she liked to eat best, when
she could have anything in the world. He didn't know what
she liked to do on a cozy winter evening, when she was
curled up by the fire. All he did know, was how she felt
when he was making love to her. How her eyes gazed into
his. And how he'd thought that if he could stay with this
woman forever, he'd be content. All he really knew was,
she felt *right* when she was in his arms. She felt right when
she was laughing with him, arguing with him, listening to
him, talking to him. She'd felt right from the beginning.
All J.D. knew was— "I love her."

He straightened up in a hurry, and pushed his hat back
as he looked up at the sky and whistled. "Well, I'll be
dipped." Then he lowered his head and directed a hard
stare at the house. "I'll be double-damned-dipped!" He
stared at the outline of his home, warm and welcoming in
the soft evening twilight. He thought of Rebecca, tucked
away inside. "I love her. I love every damned virgin Yankee inch of her."

He pulled his hat lower over his eyes, settling it firmly
on his head, in preparation for the coming battle. "If that
woman thinks she can run away from me, she's got another
think coming. She might not be a Texan yet, but by God,
she will be before I get finished with her." With his heels
digging firmly into the dust, he stalked toward the house.

After leaving J.D. and Rosalie in the barn, Rebecca
yanked open the back door of the ranch house. She paused
inside the screened-in porch to compose herself before trying to face Smoke. The ache in her heart intensified. She

didn't know how she could do it, but she needed to leave. There was no way she could stay here and tamely finish out her vacation.

Everytime she looked at J.D., she would remember seeing him, his eyes shining with what she could have sworn was love. She would remember his body, flaming with desire and slick from their lovemaking. She buried her face in her hands for a moment, trying to escape from J. D. McCoy. No use. She would remember his laughter, his tender touch with baby, Jessie—her head jerked up—his appalled reaction to a possible pregnancy and commitment to her! That's right, she told herself. *Get angry. Get angry at that tall, handsome, insensitive jerk! Remember what a gulf there is between us. He's beer and I'm champagne. He's down-home and I'm uptown. He's—here and I'm there.*

It wasn't helping.

She slammed her hand against the back screen door. Try again, Rebecca. *J. D. McCoy is nothing like the kind of man I need. He's a diversion, a one-night stand, a vacation experience. A way to shed that cloak of virginity I've been using to hide myself from the world.* Rebecca nodded, tossing her head and lifting her chin. That's better.

With teeth clenched and a determined air, Rebecca yanked open the door and stepped inside the kitchen. She stopped, astonished by the sight of a huge, younger man sitting in a chair at the end of the table. He looked like a bear! A big, old, shaggy bear. Her gaze traveled from the large head covered with long, brown hair, over the brown eyes that widened as they met hers, to the full beard that shadowed the rest of his face. A beard that made a wonderful frame for the large white teeth he suddenly bared in a wide smile. Rebecca automatically smiled back before dropping her gaze to the bundle in his arms. There, looking content and sucking avidly on a bottle, was Jessie.

"Wh—" Rebecca's voice croaked, before she recovered from her surprise. "Who on earth are you?"

"I'm Tim Enderwine, Rosalie's husband…"

Rebecca leaned back against the doorjamb. "Rosalie's what?"

"…and Jessie's father."

"You're kidding." Then Rebecca realized she must look like a perfect idiot, poised in the doorway and hanging on for dear life. Straightening her shoulders, she pushed away from the door and walked toward him. "I'm so happy to meet you."

"I'm right pleased to meet you too, Rebecca." At her surprise he grinned. "Rosalie described you. I want to thank you for taking such good care of her, and this little one, for the last few months."

Disarmed by his charming manner, Rebecca smiled. "It was a pleasure. Rosalie is quite a—"

"Handful?"

"Well, I wasn't going to say so."

Tim chuckled and removed the bottle from Jessie's mouth, then lifted the baby up over his shoulder and patted expertly. "That's all right. I can deal with her. Now that I've gone and married her." He smiled as the baby let out a loud burp and stood up. "Everything is going to be just fine from now on."

Rebecca gasped. The man towering over her must stand at least six foot six in his stocking feet. She was wrong. He wasn't just a bear, he was a bona fide grizzly! But there was a gentleness in his hands, and in the smile on his face as he looked at his little daughter that made Rebecca like him immediately, and more than that, trust him. Rosalie would be all right with this man. He would be the strong, steadying influence she needed. Instinctively, Rebecca knew, J.D. would take to him, too—eventually. After he got over his protective stance concerning his little sister.

"Are you planning on living here, at the ranch?"

Tim let out a laugh that sounded like a roar. "God bless me, no."

Rebecca glanced at Jessie, expecting her to yell at the unexpected sound. But instead of being frightened, Jessie reached up and grabbed a handful of Tim's beard. It reminded Rebecca of her behavior with J.D.'s horse earlier. "I'm a singer, Rebecca. I can't stick around here."

"A singer?" Of all the people Rosalie might have gotten involved with, an entertainer had never crossed Rebecca's mind.

"I got me a career in Nashville that's just taking off. We'll be living there for a while. Then, when my first record hits it big, I can move us back to my hometown in Texas."

"Where is your hometown?"

"Down the road a bit...near Houston."

"Houston is pretty far from here, isn't it?"

Tim grinned as he loosened Jessie's hand. "Well, we're used to thinking in terms of big. Miles, appetites, you know what I mean, ma'am? The other side of the state to some people, is just down the road a piece to a Texan."

Then it hit Rebecca. J.D. would be alone. Rosalie would go off again to her own life, and once again, J.D. would be left here on his own. A solitary figure, left alone to reflect on his past and to face the future without love by his side. The image disturbed Rebecca. J.D. might not admit it, but he needed people. She bit her lip, feeling the tears she'd been holding back with anger start to well in her eyes.

"Tim," Smoke called as he came into the kitchen from the hallway. "I put your suitcase up in Rosalie's—" He stopped and stared at Rebecca. "Well, so you're back. Have a nice ride?" Then he directed a sharp, knowing look at her.

"Mmm-hmm." Rebecca knew Smoke must have noticed

her teary expression, when he suddenly changed the subject.

"Tim, why don't you take that baby outside and set a spell in the porch swing? That young'un really likes it out there."

Tim slid a glance between the two of them, before shrugging amicably. "I wouldn't mind setting a spell myself, Smoke." With that he and Jessie left the kitchen.

Smoke turned to face Rebecca. "What's up now, missy?"

Rebecca dashed away a tear. "I tried to— We— Me and J.D.—" She tossed her head and sniffed. "It's all happening so fast Smoke. How can you trust something that happens so fast? We scarcely know each other."

"Sometimes all it takes is a look, missy. You and that boy ought to know that by now." He folded his arms across his skinny chest. "Gosh darn, I could feel the sparks shooting out like a piece of dry kindling, the first minute you two stepped into my kitchen. I knew then that I'd better get used to having you around. 'Cause you were going to be here, whether each of you knew it or not. Now it's time to quit burying your head, and go on out there. You tell that man to quit acting like a ten-year-old and not to let you get away." Smoke shook one clenched fist. "Or I'll have to give him what-for."

"I don't know if I— Maybe he— You could be wrong, you know."

"I could be, yep. But you'll never know if I'm right unless you try, will you?"

Rebecca stared at Smoke. All her life, she'd wanted a home and a figure who could become a parent. Someone who'd perform the role better than her mother and many stepfathers. But never in her wildest imaginings, did she expect the parental wisdom and sharing to come from a grizzled, old cowboy. A man who, Rebecca realized, possessed more learning and knowledge of people in his little fingertip, than all the high-powered, well-educated, proper individuals she'd ever known.

Rebecca walked over to the old cowboy. Lifting his huge hat, she leaned over and pressed a kiss on his sparsely covered head. "Smoke, I love you."

"Not me, him. Go tell J.D. He needs you." Blushing, he grabbed his hat and jammed it back down on his ears. He pulled it down so low, his eyes were scarcely visible, but they glittered fiercely.

Smoke was right, Rebecca thought. J.D. needs someone who loves him standing beside him. He needs a woman who isn't afraid to speak her mind. A woman who will yank him from his comfort zone, and make him experience new things. He needs a woman who puts her best effort against any problem that comes her way. J.D. needs—*me*. The kitchen went out of focus and then slowly came back in as the words formed in her mind. *And I need him. Oh, do I need him. I love him.*

"What are you standing there for? A body would think you're rooted to the floor." He waved his hand. "Go on, now, you get out of here and do what your heart tells ya, missy. Go out there and bag that dumb son of a buck, before I have to take a strap to him for being too ornery to know what's good for him. And too dumb to hold on to it, once he's found it."

Rebecca needed no more urging. It's what she wanted to do, anyway. Smoke just gave her the extra push. "You're right, Smoke. I'll be back after I take care of J. D. McCoy."

Rebecca barreled through the screen door, knocking into Rosalie, who was just coming in. Grabbing the younger woman by the elbows, Rebecca demanded urgently, "Rosalie, where's J.D.?"

"He's still in the barn. I wanted to talk to you and apolog—"

"Later. We'll talk later," Rebecca said, as she stepped

around Rosalie. "By the way, I like Tim." She turned, walking backward to add, "Be happy, okay?"

Rosalie glanced over Rebecca's shoulder for a moment, before dragging her gaze back and grinning. "You too, Rebecca."

"I intend to be." Rebecca turned sharply and caught sight of J.D. emerging from the barn. In the deepening twilight he looked like an image from one of her dreams. But this man was very real, as she had discovered over the past few days. She knew this man. Knew him for all time.

Rebecca paid no attention to the slamming screen door behind her that indicated Rosalie had gone back inside. She and J.D. might as well have been alone there in the Texas countryside. With a steady gait, Rebecca walked toward him. This man had better realize that he has finally met his match. There was no way she was going to cut and run and leave him. She didn't care how wrong they seemed for each other on the surface. Underneath, where it counted, this was the only man in the world for her. And she was going to convince him of that if she had to hog-tie him, mount up and drag him behind a horse to do it!

She continued to walk toward him, while he did the same. Finally they both drew to a stop about a hundred feet from each other. Time stood still.

After a moment, J.D.'s hands slowly moved to his belt. He hooked his thumbs in the leather. Unknowingly, Rebecca did the same, before the irreverent thought hit her.

We look like two gunfighters at the OK Corral, getting ready to blast each other into eternity.

She swallowed a chuckle. Well, in a way that is what's going to happen, she thought, as she looked him over. When a cowboy meets a tenderfoot and the tenderfoot wins—the shock will probably stop all the clocks in Texas. She drew her weapon at the exact same moment as J.D.

"I'm not leaving, J.D."

"You're not going, Reb."

"What did you say?" Rebecca asked J.D.

"Come again?" J.D. asked Rebecca.

"I said, I'm not leaving here. I'm not leaving you without a fight, J.D. I'm not letting you make me think you don't want me, just because you're afraid to get too close to me. Because you're afraid I'll leave. I'm not giving up on you and me. I'm made of stronger stuff than that, and by God, I'm going to prove it to you, if it takes me the rest of my life—and yours!" She placed her hands on her hips. "Now, what did you start to say?"

J.D. blinked. "I said, you're not going, Reb. You're not leaving me because you're afraid to commit to a man. 'Cause you're afraid it won't work out. That you'll be like your mother. You're nothing like your mother, from what I see. You're a fighter, a stayer. You're a woman who jumps in for the long haul. And I'll be damned if I'm going to let you quit on us, just because I said something stupid, 'cause I wasn't thinking." He shoved his hat back and completely disarmed her by giving her a grin that immediately sent shivers up and down her spine. "Hell, if you're going to leave every time I say or do something you don't like, you're going to be coming and going so often you'll wear a rut in the road."

Baffled, they both looked at each other for a second, unsure what to do next. Rebecca settled it by racing to J.D. and throwing her arms around his neck. He grabbed her, pulling her tightly against him, as if he'd never let her escape.

"I love you, J.D."

"Not as much as I love you, Reb."

Rebecca sighed. "You're going to call me Reb for the rest of my life, aren't you?"

J.D. pressed a kiss into the tender hollow under her ear. "Yep."

His laconic answer made her giggle. "Good." Pulling

his face to hers, she pressed kisses against his jaw, until he took the control away from her and found her lips.

After a long, satisfying moment, Rebecca got serious. "J.D., why did you change your mind? What about all that stuff you were saying about a baby—"

"Reb. I was behaving like a love-maddened stallion, lashing out at everything because I *wanted* you so much. I couldn't believe I'd really found you. Then I couldn't believe I'd made you mine. Me. No one else, ever had done that before. I was the first. I wanted to be the only. The thought of it overwhelmed me. All I could do was thrash in all directions, until somebody threw a noose over me."

"I know what you mean. I was running from the reality of what I thought I should want, and away from what I really did want. It didn't take me long to discover that what I needed, and have always needed is you. *You.* A man with a heart and a pride as big as the land you live on. A man to make a home with, a family with." She pressed kisses all over his face, before taking his mouth in a kiss that promised forever. Breathlessly she whispered, "I need a man who will make me face myself. Face what really matters to me. I want to make a home with you. I want to have children with you. I need you, J.D. Do you need me?"

J.D. kissed her again. This time, much as a starving man might, with his tongue slipping inside to caress hers, probing more deeply, folding her body closer to try to absorb her warmth. He drew back and stared down into her eyes. "Only for ordinary, day-to-day living. Only for waking up to in the morning, cuddling at lunch and holding on to in the evening. Only because you are the only woman who fits at my side. The only woman I could ever imagine having my babies."

Stunned by his eloquence, Rebecca pulled his face back to hers. She ran her tongue over his lips, to taste again the sweetness of what he'd just said. "Oh, J.D. That's the most poetic thing I've ever heard you say."

"What?" J.D. drew back, giving her a look that almost made her laugh. "Poetic? Me?" He grinned. "Well, hell, darlin', don't get carried away, now. I'm just a *cowboy*, remember?"

Rebecca licked her lips. "Mmm, I love cowboys."

His blue eyes twinkled, even as they warmed with desire. "In that case, I'll make sure you can always tell *this* cowboy from every other one from now on." He stroked his hands down the sides of her body. "Even in the dark, honey."

"Promise?"

"You can bet on it, sugar."

"Honey...sugar."

J.D. grinned and nibbled her ear. "I've got a sweet tooth, is all."

"Oh." Rebecca shivered as his tongue darted inside her ear, sending quivering sensations throughout her body. Much more of this and she'd throw him down on the ground right there and ride him until his eyes crossed. "If I have any good sense—"

"You'll run away?"

"Oh, no." Rebecca pressed her hand against the front of his jeans and massaged him through the fabric. "I'll get used to enjoying every minute of your sweet-talking ways." Her hand continued a downward path, darting to play with the button on his pants. She slipped the metal stud through the buttonhole as she licked his lips. "Let me show you how sweet I can be, sugar."

Eagerly he stroked his fingers over her zipper. "I will, honey. Every hour of every day."

Rebecca melted against him as he started to inch the zipper down so he could slip a finger inside to stroke her flushed skin. "If it gets much hotter out here, I'll melt into a puddle right at your feet."

J.D. withdrew his hand and hers before lifting her high into his arms. "I can think of much better things for that beautiful body to do.'' He pressed her close against his chest, and strode toward the barn.

Rebecca roused herself from her sensual haze. ''Why are we going to the barn?''

''I'm so hot I'm about to explode and the house is too far away.'' J.D. toed open the door, and kicked it shut behind them. He strode across the floor to a stack of bales at the back of the barn. ''I'm going to show you the fine art of making love in a haystack.''

Rebecca caressed his ear with her tongue. ''Aren't we ever going to use a bed?''

''We'll get there, darlin'. Eventually.''

Gently, he placed her in the sweet-smelling straw and followed her down. ''Now, pay attention.''

Rebecca shivered as his body covered hers. ''I think I should warn you, cowboy. I'm a slow learner.''

He unhooked her bra and lowered his head. ''That's all right, sugar. I'm a slow teacher. And if it takes the rest of our lives, I'm going to teach you all the ways we make love in Texas.''

* * * * *

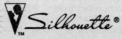

If you enjoyed what you just read,
then we've got an offer you can't resist!

Take 2 bestselling love stories FREE!

Plus get a FREE surprise gift!

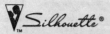
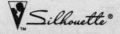